The Case of the Missing Dinosaur Egg

June Whyte

A Chiana Ryan Mystery

*The Case of the
Missing Dinosaur Egg*
June Whyte

A Chiana Ryan Mystery

This edition published by Picarones Press
A division of Misti Media LLC
https://www.mistimedia.com
Available in both Paperback and eBook Editions
1 2 3 4 5 6 7 8 9 10

Paperback ISBN: 978-1-969139-93-2
eBook ISBN: 978-1-969139-92-5

This is a work of fiction. The characters, dialogue and events in this book are wholly fictional, and any resemblance to companies and actual persons, living or dead, is purely coincidental

1

The museum smelled of dust. Of old things. Of dry stuffed animals with blank staring eyes. It was our school end-of-term excursion and our teacher was herding us through the South Australian Museum—'to enrich our lives, by observing how others lived in the past'.

They're Ms Winters—our year seven teacher's words— not mine.

My name is Chiana Ryan and I'm more into solving mysteries and writing stories, than studying dead things. Although we, (that's me and my best friend, Tayla) *did* stumble across a dead body while solving our last mystery. And we, (that's me, Tayla, Jack, Sarah and my goof-off bulldog, Leroy) *did* come close to being made dead ourselves when the bad guys kidnapped us.

I sighed, a long drawn-out sigh. My best friend, Tayla, who is normally sane and fun to be with, was babbling on about horses. Yeah, horses. You know, those biting, kicking, hairy things that bolt, rear, buck or just plain lie down on top of you—just for the fun of it. And after trying unsuccessfully to shut Tayla up, I was opting whether to dump her in a mummy case, or ask my buddy, Jack, to help me lock her in with the stuffed crocodiles.

What a swizz! She'd read two horse magazines the night before and today she was an expert on the subject.

I turned to Jack who was dead keen on museum stuff. All elbows and knees, Jack towered over me by a good five inches. His short spiky red hair stuck up like porcupine quills. Probably forgot to comb it when he got out of bed this morning. His light blue school shirt had a damp stain on the front that looked suspiciously like milk from his morning bowl of Weeties.

"Hey, Jack, aren't these shrunken heads something else?" I asked, pointing to a large glass case full of wooden spears, clubs, nose decorations and human heads. The heads were black and shrunken to the size of large fists.

Jack McEvoy's blue eyes widened as he peered closer at the grisly exhibit.

"Wow!" he breathed. "Says here these heads are over three hundred years old. People sure had cool hobbies back then. More fun than collecting stamps."

I'd been hoping to distract Tayla with the shrunken heads—but no luck. Her eyes, still glazed over with horsy zeal, didn't even flicker in the direction of the glass case. Instead, she linked arms with me.

"Isn't it great your mum saying I can go with you and Sarah for the holidays? Did you know she rung Sarah's Aunt Kate and arranged it for us?"

"Mmmm..." I mumbled with about as much

enthusiasm as a snail lining up for a race with a greyhound.

My mum and step-father, Ken, had decided to go on a belated honeymoon, which was okay with me. After all, they'd been married for six months and deserved some time together. But I'd counted on spending those two weeks with Tayla—at her place—doing cool stuff like playing computer-games and painting our toe-nails green and jumping off the Semaphore jetty and swimming in the sea and practicing our sleuthing skills in case another mystery popped up just begging to be solved. Not shoveling smelly horse-poo at a riding school. And definitely not with my pain-in-the-place-you-sit-on step-sister, Sarah, and a step-Aunt I'd never even met.

Why did Tayla have to go and spoil everything?

Geez, if a stray dog glanced at Tayla, she'd turn a vomit shade of yellow. If a hairy spider came within eye-balling distance of her, she'd break the two minute mile running away. Yet she wanted to spend our precious school holidays with biting, kicking, snorting horses.

And what was worse—she was dragging me along too.

Suddenly, *you-know-who* smiled and punched me on the arm. "Hey, come on sour-puss. This holiday will be fun."

Fun? I scowled my meanest dragon scowl. "I don't like horses."

My friend put on her snooty look, the one she usually keeps for scabby boys and little kids who annoyed her. Through squinty eyes I watched her hitch up her navy school skirt—all the better to show off her picture perfect legs—and toss her fairy-tale curly blonde hair from her eyes.

"Chiana," she said in her best grown-up voice. "The best way to overcome fear is to confront it."

Aaaarrrggggghhh!

My normally fun best friend sounded like she'd swallowed the self-help book we'd borrowed from the library the week before. I glared my frustration. "I never said I was *afraid* of horses—I just don't like them!"

"Oh. So how come you fainted when that policeman's horse brushed up against you in last year's Christmas pageant?"

"Tayla, it was forty-two degrees in the shade that day. People were dropping like flies after a 'Sprayathon'. Or didn't you notice?"

"Whatever."

I turned away, hopping mad. Perhaps I could talk Mum into letting me stay home on my own while they went on their belated honeymoon.

In the Egyptian Room, while everyone else *oohed* and *aahhed* over the tombs and embalmed mummies—like poor Renpit-Nefert who died and got herself wrapped in bandages about two and a half thousand years ago—Tayla rambled on about horse-feeds.

In the Kauri room, while we were supposed to be taking notes on aboriginal artifacts, Tayla described every stitch of the new two-toned jodhpurs her mum bought her the day before.

"Probably be three-toned after you hit the ground a few times," I mumbled as we followed the class through the doorway and toward everyone's favorite museum display, the 120 million year old opalesced fossil, *Addyman Plesiosaur.*

The enormity of this specimen even shut Tayla up. A sign in front of the monster said this was the largest and most complete dinosaur ever found and although it represented a new species, couldn't be named because important parts of the skeleton were missing.

I hugged my bag to my body and looked up at the huge reconstructed figure towering above us. Even though it was only made of bones wired together, the prehistoric monster was scary enough to make me shiver in the warmth of the central heating. Fancy having one of those ugly critters chasing after you waving a knife and fork. Made horses seem almost cuddly.

At the bottom of the display a fossilized dinosaur egg, proclaiming to have the embryo of a *Therizinosaur* inside perched on its special stand. I stared sadly at the dirty grey egg which was about 3½" round and thought: Poor little guy—didn't even get to be born.

The egg wobbled.

I squished my eyes shut, opened them again, and stared.

The egg stared right back at me.

I shook my head and blinked. Perhaps Tayla was sending me crazy and making me see things that weren't really there.

Evidently tired of getting no response from me, Tayla turned to Jack and was raving on to him.

"What about you, Jack?" she asked. "I bet *you're* looking forward to our holiday. Sarah's Aunt Kate says we get a horse of our own to look after and ride. She also said on the last day we'll be competing in something called a Team Cross-Country event."

"Yeah, should be fun," answered Jack, his eyes still glued to the monster stack of bones in front of us. "I can't get there for the first week though. Have to play in the footy finals on Saturday."

"Why?"

"Tayla, give it a rest," I growled, still surveying the sneaky egg. "Of course Jack has to play in the finals. He's their best player and also the team captain."

And then the egg moved again.

It rocked from side to side as though the prehistoric baby inside was getting ready to burst out of its shell.

I took a long step backwards. After so many millions of years without food I reckoned Baby Dino would have to be starving and I had no intention of being the first course on his menu.

"Did you see that?" I whispered, grabbing Tayla by the arm.

"See what?"

"That dinosaur egg moved. I think it's going to hatch."

Both Tayla and Jack looked at me as though I had

suddenly sprouted an extra nose.

"Dinosaur eggs can't move," said Jack. "Or hatch."

"They can't do anything," added Tayla trying to pull her arm from my death-grip. "They're fossilized."

Before I could argue, a muscly guy dressed in a maroon and yellow uniform, like a museum curator, came barreling into the room. He crashed into me, then, without a word of apology, kept going—as though knocking a school-girl in the stomach with his elbow and scattering her notes over the floor was all in a day's work.

Tayla goggled, while Jack bent down to pick up my notes.

"Did that creep hurt you?" he asked handing the papers back to me.

"Nah. I'm okay."

I turned around, ready to tell the human whirlwind what I thought of him, but he was gone. I'd remember him though. Thin face, greasy dark hair, garlicky breath and an elbow sharpened to a pencil point.

I frowned in concentration. "You know, Jack, I don't think that guy's a museum worker at all. I reckon he's a fake."

"You could be right." Jack looked thoughtful. "I wonder why he was in such a hurry."

"Get a move on you three." Ms Winters—or *Frosty*, as we called her—poked her long nose through the doorway. "We're waiting for you. The rest of the class is in the cafeteria waiting to order lunch and discuss their individual projects."

While Tayla and Jack headed for the doorway, I gave the sneaky *Therizinosaur* another quick study.

Statue-still.

I shook my head.

Right…

After bundling my notebook into my backpack I turned to follow the others—glanced over my shoulder one last time—and found the egg slowly and silently lifting into the air.

My eyes spun. My brain switched off. I opened my mouth to call out to Jack and Tayla, but although the words formed, no sound came out. And by the time my voice pushed through my clogged up throat and reached my lips, the egg had disappeared through a hole in the ceiling.

Holy catfish! I blinked. Scanned the empty room. Craned my neck backwards to get a better view of the pale yellow ceiling.

What was going on here? How could a mega-million-year-old dinosaur egg suddenly up and vanish?

Finally, Jack poked his head through the doorway and woke me from my daze.

"Come on, Cha," he called out. "Frosty says if you're not in the canteen in two minutes she'll deduct marks off your project."

"Jack! Look! The dinosaur egg! It—it's gone!"

Jack walked slowly toward me, his eyes wary.

"Cha?"

"Stop looking at me as if I'm crazy. See for yourself. The little *Therizinosaur* has disappeared."

Jack frowned down at the display. The plaque was still there—'*Fossilized Dinosaur Egg discovered by Professor Cyril Goodenough on 8th September 1934*'—but the stand itself was empty.

"Wow!" breathed Jack, getting excited and going a plum shade of red. "Did you see where it went?"

"It was like a magician's trick. The egg just seemed to rise in the air—then disappear."

"Wow!" repeated Jack, his eyes wide and his feet dancing on the spot as he gazed at the ceiling.

I reached for my backpack.

"Time to take notes," I whispered, dragging out a notebook and my favorite silver colored pen.

Excitement sizzled through me like a lightning bolt as I opened at a fresh page and jotted down the important facts so far:

CASE OF THE DISAPPEARING DINOSAUR EGG

1. Egg wobbled on its stand.
2. Rose in the air like magic.
3. Disappeared through the ceiling.

"A new mystery?" whispered Jack, eyes shining like just-minted twenty cent coins.

I nodded, feeling an excited grin spread across my face. "Yeah. And what do you know…it's fallen right into our laps."

2

It was in all the papers.

'*Valuable fossilized dinosaur egg disappears from State Museum.*'

There was even a blurry picture of me standing beside the giant *Addyman Plesiosaur*. I looked stiff and dorky. Like something from the museum displays. Like something that had been dead and stuffed for a couple of centuries.

The caption underneath read: '*Schoolgirl stands and watches while valuable egg disappears.*'

Holy catfish! What did they expect me to do? Throw on my Super-Cha cape and fly through the air to save the egg?

At least with the disappearance of the dinosaur egg I had another mystery to solve. Now I could write a second true crime story about the amazing but fictitious Private Investigator, Rebecca Turnbull and her vicious Doberman, Fang.

Earlier this year I'd won a true-crime writing competition for children under fourteen and now the online *Kidlit* magazine wanted to publish more of my work.

Okay. All I had to do was solve the egg-mystery and I could write another story.

Unfortunately, a couple of things stopped me from putting on my P.I. sunnies and trench-coat.

One—there was very little in the way of clues. The police said the burglars must have lassoed the egg with a near-invisible wire then hauled it up through a small hole they'd cut in the roof. After that, both egg and thieves had disappeared without a trace.

But what really got me spitting was the second problem. As we private investigators say—I couldn't follow up on my investigations. How could I follow up on anything? For the next two weeks I'd be spending every minute of every day either shoveling food into one end of a horse or shoveling what came out the other end.

But I'm getting ahead of myself.

On arriving home from the museum, Mum was out front waiting for me. Which was unusual. Normally she's in the kitchen getting dinner ready. *Wonder what's up?* I thought as I shut the gate and walked up the path. Deep wrinkles ran up each side of Mum's nose, jumped over her eyes and burrowed into her forehead. Hmm…guess she wasn't waiting to give me a banana and fudge flavored ice-cream cone.

"Chiana Elizabeth Ryan!"

Uh! Oh! Definitely no ice-cream cone.

"What's this about you getting involved in a burglary at

the museum?"

"Hardly," I protested as I walked past Mum and threw my back-pack on the hall table before zeroing in on the kitchen and the huge cottage-shaped biscuit jar. "I just saw the dinosaur egg disappear. That's all."

A delta cream biscuit half-way to my mouth, I stopped, puzzled. "Anyway, how did you know so soon? Did Ms Winters ring?"

And then I spotted my step-sister, Sarah, perched on a kitchen stool, glass of milk in one hand, vegemite sandwich in the other.

Of course!

Blabbermouth!

"Couldn't wait, could you?"

"Nope!"

"Why didn't you let *me* tell Mum what happened?"

Sarah shrugged—all couldn't care less. "More fun this way," she said then grinned this real crocodile grin and I swear her pearly white teeth looked like they'd been sharpened to vampire points.

Recently Sarah and I made a sort of truce. We'd agreed to *try* to get along. *Try* to live in the same house without blowing each other up. But six months of arguing and getting up each other's nose made it a shaky truce.

Although the same age—*almost thirteen*—Sarah and I were way different. Sarah was chocolate. I was licorice-allsorts. Sarah's fair hair hung smugly down her back like silvery silk. My thick reddish coppery hair, although long, often frizzed and stood on end like it had been plugged into an electric socket then turned up to high. Sarah dressed like Miss Teen Australia. I wore knee-less jeans and whatever T-shirt jumped out of the drawer into my hand each morning.

Ever since Sarah found out we were spending the holidays at her Aunt Kate's, she'd been rabbiting on—talking big. You know, about what a mega horse-rider she was. Before the age of ten—which is when she'd discovered nail-polish and Sherpa fashion statements—she'd evidently spent every holiday at her Aunt Kate's riding school.

Probably jumping her horse over sky-scrapers and leaping swollen rivers in one bound.

All I could say was: Huh! If Sarah was a whiz at this stupid horse-riding stuff—it must be dead easy.

Mum followed me into the kitchen. She stood by the door, hands on hips, one toe tapping rhythmically on the multi-colored linoleum floor.

"Chiana, I don't want you getting involved in any more mysteries. Last time you worried me so much I ended up with a dozen new grey hairs."

"*Muuum,*" I began, hooking a second delta cream from the biscuit barrel then fixing her with my best imitation of a sensible grown-up daughter. "I'm not *involved* in anything! All I did was stand there and watch while a dinosaur egg disappeared through the ceiling."

I took a bite out of my biscuit and kept talking, my voice

sounding a bit muffled. "Now, about me going with Sarah to her Aunt Kate's while you and Ken go on your honeymoon…" I locked eyes with mum, pleadingly. "Why can't I stay here? Please…"

"Don't be silly, Cha. I can't leave you at home on your own."

"I wouldn't be on my own. I'd have Leroy to protect me."

Sarah's snort echoed around the kitchen like a trumpeting elephant. I sent a knife-edged glare in her direction before turning back to Mum.

"Well, what about Mrs. Potter next door? If anything happened—and it won't—I could always call her."

"Mrs. Potter is deaf, Chiana and she's already looking after Cat."

"Mum, I'm not a baby anymore. I'm *almost* thirteen."

"Thirteen?" she scoffed. "When I was thirteen I still had to ask my parents' permission to go to the corner shop."

"But that was back in the olden days when—"

I caught sight of Mum's bulldog scowl and decided not to continue.

"I can't leave you without adult supervision, Chiana. I'd be ringing home ten times a day. Think about it…Ken and I have been married for six months and only now are we going on our honeymoon. Naturally we want to relax and enjoy some quality time together. Is that too much to ask?"

"Of course not, Mum." I drew myself up to my full height of five foot one and seven-eighths. "You know I'm happy for you and Ken. It's just that I'm not real keen on horses. And now there's this new mystery with the egg to—"

"That's it!" Mum grabbed the kitchen knife and started chopping potatoes like they were a mob of cold-eyed, nasty-looking bad-guys—all intent on kidnapping and torturing me until I told them every one of the country's classified secrets. "You haven't been listening, Chiana. I said you're *not* getting involved in another mystery."

Me and my big mouth.

I took a quick step backwards as one very large potato hurled itself off the work bench in fright, just missing Mum's knife as it crashed downwards.

"Look what happened last time you decided to play the detective," Mum continued, grabbing the errant potato and murdering it before throwing the evidence in the pot. "You and Sarah and your friends almost got killed. No, Chiana. There's no way Ken and I could relax on the Gold Coast knowing you were putting your nose where it might get blown off. You're going to Kate's riding-school and that's final."

"But Mum—"

"But nothing! Tayla's mother has kindly offered to drive the three of you to *Treehaven Stables* tomorrow morning so we can catch our plane at one. I want you packed and ready to leave when they come. Is that clear?"

Mum must have seen the anxiety in my eyes because her voice softened. "Come on, Cha. Ken and I want to enjoy our holiday—not worry about you. If you're at Kate's while we're away, we'll know you're safe."

"Safe?" My mother throws me to a pack of wild horses then says I'll be safe.

I stomped up the stairs, pausing outside my bedroom door to offer half a delta cream to my roly-poly bulldog who was sprawled legs in the air, tongue dangling.

Just as his slobbering jaws opened to receive the treat, Mum's voice crashed through the air and bounced off the walls.

"And don't feed Leroy your biscuit."

Grrrrrrrrrrrrr…

"The vet put him on a diet," she continued in a voice loud enough for the entire street to hear. "He said you could have killed him with all those chocolate Tim Tams. While we're away he's been booked into a boarding-kennel where they'll make sure he stays on the diet."

Leroy curled both paws over his head and whined pitifully. Leaning down I rubbed his tummy.

"Poor Leroy," I commiserated. "I know exactly how you feel."

3

The tires on Neil's red Monaro hummed hypnotically as we followed the grey ribbon of road on the way to *Treehaven Stables*.

Instead of Tayla's mum driving, it was her latest dreadlocked, vegetarian boyfriend who sat behind the wheel of the car, while she, dressed in black leather, curled up in the passenger's seat beside him. Sarah, Tayla and I shared the back seat with riding boots, horse-magazines, suede chaps, riding helmets and anything else that wouldn't fit into our cases.

For the last half hour we'd played a dreary game of Sevens. Tayla was too wired to concentrate. Sarah was itching to start an argument. And I kept thinking about the missing dinosaur egg and kept playing the wrong card.

Bored, and wishing I was at home, I yawned and flicked a casual glance through the open car window.

My mouth still in mid-yawn…I froze in disbelief at the view.

For there, pulling out of a rutted driveway onto the roadway, grey smoke billowing around it like a winter mist, was a battered grey utility. And it was heading straight for our car.

"Look out!"

My warning was lost in a screech of tires and the clatter of boots, cards and helmets as they sprayed into the air and onto the floor.

Neil stamped on his brakes, wrenched the car sideways and let out a string of explosive four-letter words that left my eardrums ringing. The driver of the rusty grey ute with the words, *Professor T. Goodenough*, painted in heritage green on the passenger side door, also braked, then looked vaguely around, like a sheep separated from its flock.

For a couple of seconds—time stood still.

I could see this skinny old man hunched behind the wheel. He sat there, a dreamy look on his face. His white hair straggled onto his shoulders. His long beard, like tangled barbwire, rested in his lap. And then, without warning, he crunched the gears and his car leap-frogged forward again.

Neil's ear-splitting roar broke the spell. "You stupid imbecile!" Caught in the act of taking off, Neil slammed his foot on the brake again. "The man's a moron!"

Now tootling along in front of us, the ute stalled, coughed, spluttered, then hiccupped forward with a deafening bang.

Once more Neil's shiny red Monaro slithered and fishtailed across the road. My fingers, now in the shape of eagle's talons, dug into the leather upholstery as though attempting to rip the driver's seat from the floor.

"What's happening?" gasped Tayla her face the color of sour milk.

As our car came to rest on the verge of the road, my step-sister, Sarah, rubbed at a red mark on her forehead, where she'd been crowned by a flying missile.

"Ooowwch!" she whined, her bottom lip trembling. "That *really* hurt!"

Confused, I stared at the property Professor Goodenough's car had come from. Grass and weeds ran riot between the trees. And the driveway was full of ruts, so deep, cows could disappear into them and never be seen again.

But what really caught my eye were the roughly painted signs. They were everywhere. Stuck in the ground—nailed to trees—wired onto fence posts. And all painted in this grisly shade of blood red.

What was it with this guy?

"Everyone okay back there?" Tayla's mum peered over into the back seat. She must have been touching up her lipstick when the car braked because there was a vivid streak of red that ran up one side of her nose. Except for the ugly red slash, her face was whiter than her daughter's.

"I feel sick," moaned Tayla.

"Me too," sniveled Sarah.

"What about you, Cha?"

My mind whirled as I studied the writing on the signs. 'Do Not Enter'. 'Danger'. 'Vicious Bull—eats People'.

'Trespassers Shot on Sight'.

"Cha?"

I blinked at Tayla's mum then nodded my head at the bewildering signs. "That old guy seems a bit unfriendly, doesn't he?"

"Bit crazy you mean," Tayla grumped, winding down the window and taking great gulps of fresh air.

"He's stark raving bonkers!" Neil started the car again. He checked the rear-vision mirror before edging back onto the road and driving slowly in the direction of *Treehaven Stable,* which was only a hundred meters further up the road.

Wiping the lipstick from her nose with a scrunched up tissue, Tayla's mum said, "I want you girls to promise not to go anywhere near that horrible place while you're staying here."

"Mum—are you for real?" Tayla gave an eye-roll and shook her head. "Nothing short of an earthquake would get me inside that mad-man's front gate."

I didn't answer.

The old guy in the ute might look vague, almost dreamy, but there was something weird going on. What was he trying to hide? Why didn't he want people on his property? I could feel my detective's nose twitching and itching, preparing itself for a gargantuan sneeze—a sure sign of a mystery in the air. I couldn't wait to dig out my notebook and write down the important points of this new case. In my mind I could even see the opening paragraph of the new Rebecca Turnbull P.I. mystery I'd write for *Kidlit* magazine…

Φ

Rebecca Turnbull slid her right hand into the deep pocket of her trench coat feeling for the cold hard metal of her trusty snub-nosed revolver.

"Trespassers shot on sight? Vicious bull – eats people? Ha! Bring them on", she growled.

The private investigator business had slowed to a crawl lately and she and her slavering Doberman, Fang, were edgy. They couldn't wait to take on a people-eating bull or a gun-toting psychopath—whichever came along first.

Φ

As Neil's car pulled up in front of a large rambling old country house surrounded by tall trees and white fenced paddocks, I flipped my mind back to the present. *Treehaven Stables* looked okay—and would look better if they'd ship all their horses to the forests of Transylvania. Taking a deep breath, I pushed the helmet and riding boot off my lap and slowly opened the car door.

Okay, I'd left one unsolved mystery behind at the museum—but with the hint of another mystery around the corner—perhaps these holidays weren't going to be such a complete waste of time after all.

4

Fat horses—skinny horses—wild, woolly horses that looked like they'd been crossed with prehistoric mammoths.

Treehaven Stables had them all.

There was even a dog-sized horse with a polka-dot bow tied to his mane running loose. The little monster tried to pinch my notebook while I carried my luggage from the car to the house.

Big and rambling, with a verandah all around, and umpteen dozen windows, the house was surrounded by giant ghost gums. A flock of yellow-crested white cockatoos perched on the branches, arguing noisily.

"Brilliant house," said Tayla as we trudged up to a wire screened front door with a colorful wooden horse motif nailed on each side.

"My Aunt Kate bought *Treehaven* about fifteen years ago," Sarah informed us with a flick of her golden hair. "Before that it was a juvenile detention center for bad boys."

I soon found out that Sarah's Aunt Kate continued to

run the place like a detention center. Every excuse I came up with to avoid actually *getting on* a horse was shot down like tin ducks in sideshow alley. When I said I had a headache, she offered me a headache tablet. When I said I was going to chuck up, she raised one eyebrow and pointed to the passage leading to the bathroom. Talk about treating me like a naughty five-year-old trying to get out of eating her spinach.

So…two hours later, still muttering and grumbling and making excuses, I dragged my boots, toes first, through the dirt, heading for the stable. Yeah. You guessed it. I'd been summoned to the torture chamber by Kick-ass Kate.

The closer I came to the stables, the more rubbery my legs felt. Now I knew how those poor French aristocrats must have felt on their way to the guillotine. Of course Tayla had breezed through her first riding-lesson half an hour earlier and was so wired she was still gabbing away like a toy with a new battery. 'Kate said this,' and 'Angel, my pony, did that,' and 'Can't wait till I'm allowed to canter.'

Suddenly, I had an idea. Perhaps if I tripped and broke my wrist I'd get out of riding over the holidays. Nah. Kate would probably laugh, strap my wrist up with fencing wire and throw me up on the horse anyway.

I let out a long sigh.

I could see Kate waiting, long whip at the ready, in the middle of a large sandy round-yard. She was dressed in knee-high leather riding boots, hip-hugging black and white check jodhpurs and a snowy white shirt. What with her china-doll face and long silky smug-looking hair, she could have been my step-sister Sarah in twenty or thirty years' time.

Beside her, tied to the fence, was an ancient horse that looked as though it had died a couple of weeks before and no-one had noticed. Its head drooped, its woolly off-white hair stood on end and its eyes were glued shut.

"Ready, Chiana?" Kate Peterson, white teeth gleaming in the sunlight, smiled as she untied the horse from the rail and dragged its head up off the ground.

"Hey, don't bother waking him up,' I said. 'Let him sleep. I don't mind if we give riding a miss for today."

"No, no. Shakespeare's been retired for a number of years now but I'm sure he won't mind. The horse you were assigned to has an abscess in its hoof—so Shakespeare's filling in."

"Shakespeare?"

That figured. The horse looked old enough to have taken part in the original Midsummer Night's Dream.

Reluctantly I took the hard white riding helmet Tayla handed me, shoved it on over my untamable copper-colored hair and fastened the safety strap under my chin.

"Now, Cha, before we begin the lesson, I want you to give your horse a good strong pat on the neck. Let him know who's boss."

Not likely. If he finds out who's boss—I'm dead meat!

"Chiana, pat your horse."

"Whatever."

Expecting to lose at least one finger, I inched my hand nervously toward Shakespeare and tickled him behind his left ear. The hair felt soft, his ears warm. Instead of chomping my hand off at the elbow, his eyes shut fast again and I swear he purred like a cat.

"Are you sure this horse won't collapse if I sit on him?"

"Don't worry about Shakespeare—he's stronger than he looks. Now, up you go. It's time to enjoy the thrill of riding. There's nothing like it to get the adrenalin pumping."

Kate grabbed hold of my left leg in a grip that proved pushing a dirty great wheelbarrow full of horse-manure was a much better muscle-building exercise than working out at a gym. She threw me high in the air.

High in the air—over the top of the saddle—and down the other side.

Aaaaaaaaaaargh!

It was like some slapstick comedy routine from a dumb black and white television re-run. Only this was for real. Sprawled on the ground, one arm elbow-deep in a squashy pile of fresh, warm, oozing horse-manure, I could definitely vouch for how real it was.

With a furtive glance to check that no-one other than Tayla was watching, I looked straight into the grinning face of Noah Peterson, horse-rider extraordinaire. Noah had won the Junior Show jumping Championship at last year's Royal Adelaide Show. And being Kate's son, everyone at *Treehaven* treated him like he could walk on water.

Everyone but me.

"One word, Noah Peterson, and you're snail-bait," I snarled from the corner of my mouth.

His answering grin almost broke his face in two. Of all the people to witness my red-faced embarrassment—why did it have to be Noah?

Face on fire, I hurled a full-on, force-ten, mega-mean scowl in the enemy's direction. Instead of scuttling back to his hole like he was supposed to, Noah swung himself up onto the round-yard fence. Then, still grinning, he settled down, legs swinging, sunglasses perched on his nose—all the better to watch the circus.

Grrrrrrrrrrrrrrrr.

"Come on Chiana, stop playing games, and wipe that muck off your arm," Kate ordered, handing me an old sack that smelt like it had been used to wipe down a family of wet dogs. "I'm not here to give you flying lessons, you know. Next time, grab the saddle or the horse's mane and pull yourself on."

Now she tells me...

On the second try, I grabbed at handfuls of Shakespeare's stringy moth-eaten mane, praying the hair wouldn't come out in my hands. With a final weight-lifter's push from Kate, I heaved myself into the saddle and held on so tightly every knuckle went white, pink, blue and then back to white again.

"Off you go." Kate clipped a lunge line onto

Shakespeare's bridle and walked to the middle of the ring. "A couple of circles at a trot will do to start with."

A couple of circles of 'staying on' would do to start with.

I glanced first at Tayla, who gave me the thumbs-up sign, then at Noah who sat talking into his mobile phone. Probably discussing children's rights with the Prime Minister of Australia.

Okay—this was it. Time to 'face my fears', as Tayla's self-help books would say. I took a deep breath and clenched my teeth so hard it's a wonder they didn't develop hairline cracks and slowly crumble. Then, letting my deep breath out in a whoosh, I patted the hairy neck in front of me and politely asked Shakespeare to go.

Nothing happened.

In fact, I'd known rocks that were more active than the Ghost of Christmas Past who was snoring beneath me.

"No, that's not how you do it," growled Kate, flicking her long black lunging whip in the direction of the horse's rear end. "Garn, get up you lazy old fox."

With a grumpy glare and a half-hearted kick in Kate's direction, Shakespeare set off around the sandy ring at a ragged trot.

A trot that jarred every bone in my body.

A trot that made my teeth rattle like jellybeans in a jar.

A trot that threatened to shake off any body-part that wasn't screwed on tight.

"Good girl!" yelled my instructor, her dazzling grin set like cement. "Now see if you can rise up and down to the trot. Count in time. One-two. Up-down. One-two. Up-down."

"I c-c-c-can't."

My teeth rattled and clanked together, a cacophony of noise inside my head. Whenever Shakespeare went up—I hit the saddle with a loud thwack.

"Yes you can,' Kate insisted. "And look as though you're enjoying yourself, dear."

She had to be kidding…

"Now Cha, when I say up—put your weight in the stirrups and stand up. When I say down—sit softly in the saddle again. Okay?"

"C-c-can w-w-we s-s-stop n-n-now?"

If I bounced around much longer the corn-flakes I'd eaten for breakfast would be decorating Shakespeare's mane, like tinsel.

"Concentrate, dear. Up, down. Up, down. Up, down."

"Ouch! I b-b-bit my t-t-tongue!"

"Up, down. Up, down.

"I'll n-never e-ever—" I gasped. "Hey, I got that one right!"

"Good girl. Keep going. That's the way. Easy, isn't it?"

And it was. I could stand in the stirrups then sit down again in perfect time to Shakespeare's trot. It was cool. It was amazing. It was fun.

Up, down. Up, down.

A grin spread across my face. The buzz of success galloped with a crazy beat through my bloodstream and kept time with the rhythm of the trot. I leant forward to pat Shakespeare on the neck, missed his neck and somehow, not sure how, did a slow slithering somersault and hit the ground.

Kaaaaa…thud!

This was followed by a long agonizing breathy silence. I peered up from under the peak of my helmet. Was there a conspiracy going on here? Not only were Tayla, Noah and Kate grinning like a team-ad for family dental-care, but there was even a smirk on the horse's face.

I clenched my already aching teeth in a snarl fit to scare the spout off a teapot and jumped to my feet.

"Okay, you…you…*thing* you," I growled, locking eyes with the grinning horse. "It's time we got one thing straight here. I'm the boss. I'm the chief. The big Kahoona." I gave him a noisy slap on the neck just to make sure he got my drift. "And I say we try that trotting stuff one more time. Right?"

"Dunno whether that'd be a good move." Noah banged his boots against the wooden fence as he spoke.

I eyeballed him but didn't answer.

"See, we have rules here at *Treehaven*," he went on, his voice smoother than the chocolate on a Mars bar. "If someone falls off their horse they have to take a dare from the Dare-Box."

I frowned. Dare box? What was this scabby, pip-squeak raving on about now?

"You've already come off twice today so you're facing the Double-Dare box. One more fall and you win the jackpot." He tipped his head to one side, dangled his tongue from the side of his mouth like an idiot. "Whoooooo!" he moaned, all scary-like. "Who knows what dangers are hidden in the *Triple-Dare* box?"

I must have looked like a fish in a goldfish-bowl as I opened my mouth to give him a blast—couldn't think of anything mean enough to say—so closed it again.

Before climbing back on Shakespeare, I stood and watched Noah swagger off to the stables.

Short. Dark. And totally irritating.

And one to watch out for if I didn't want to land in more trouble.

5

I gazed at the baggy green canvas thing puddling at my feet. Okay, I knew it was a horse rug. I also knew it belonged to Shakespeare because Kate's last words before she shut the stable door and walked off were "…and don't forget to put Shakespeare's rug on when you've finished brushing him."

Duh…

I'd also worked out that wrapping Shakespeare in this heavy piece of canvas was a good idea because:

(a) With his bony old body he'd probably feel embarrassed without a coat.

(b) It was a good way to get his sticking-up hair to lay down flat.

(c) Old people feel the cold so I guess old horses do too.

Determined to succeed in my mission this time, I grabbed the rug firmly in both hands and heaved it in the direction of Shakespeare's back.

If only I knew which end was up.

Still munching chaff, Shakespeare lifted his nose from the feed bin, twisted his ancient head around and gave me this long-suffering, *God-you're-such-an-idiot* eye-roll. Still not sure if he'd got his message across, he let out a deep sigh, then went back to his main purpose in life— eating.

"Do you want a hand with that?"

I stiffened at Noah's voice behind me.

"No. I'm managing fine, thank you," I replied, watching the evil piece of green canvas slide off the horse's back and onto the stable floor for the third time in sixty seconds.

No way was I asking *Short Dark and Irritating* for help. Okay, I might be close to chopping the dumb rug into sixty thousand pieces and burying the remains in the manure pile, but no way would I ask for his help.

"That's not how you do it," Noah growled, opening the stable door and coming inside. "Here, I'll throw the rug on and you can do up the straps."

Well—if he put it that way. With a resigned shrug I stood back and watched Noah hoist the stubborn piece of green canvas into the air and flick it over Shakespeare's back. No fuss. Easy peasy. As simple as eating an ice-cream cone.

As he straightened the rug, he twisted two leather straps through the horse's back legs and fastened them.

"Can you at least do up the front end?" he snapped, as though talking to someone who needed a 'Horse-care for Dummies' book.

"Mmmmggg," I grunted. Perhaps I could accidentally jump up and down on his foot with the heel of my riding boot—say, six or seven times.

While I fastened Shakespeare's chest strap, Noah picked up a cardboard box he'd left in the corner of the stable and moved toward me. I scurried backwards. If a ferret or a big hairy spider jumped out of that box, Noah Peterson was deader than dead meat.

"Now," he said, shaking the box under my nose. "It's time for you to choose a Double Dare."

Aaaahhhhhh!

"I'm not choosing one of your pathetic dares, Noah. So, get lost."

"It's the rules."

"So? It used to be a rule for Eskimos to put girl-babies out in the snow to die before they realized they needed women more than they needed men."

"You're afraid."

"Afraid of what?" I bleated. "Playing Double-Dares is kid's stuff!"

"Admit it, you're afraid."

I shook my head and patted Shakespeare's scrawny neck then tried to push past Noah to get out of the stable.

"So," he continued cementing himself to the door and making it impossible for me to get past. "Do you want everyone to know you chickened out? That Sarah's stepsister and my step-cousin is a great big wuss?"

"A wuss?"

No-one called Chiana Ryan, schoolgirl P.I., winner of a real-life crime-writing competition, a wuss...

I dug my hand into the cardboard box so hard my fingers almost went straight through the bottom.

"Here," I yelled, snatching a screwed up piece of paper from amongst the others and thrusting it into his face. "You're the one who's totally freaked out with this double-dare stuff. Me—I played more grown-up games when I was in nappies."

"So you'll do it?"

I shrugged.

"Whatever."

With a smirk that had me digging my nails into the palms of both hands, Noah slowly flattened out the paper and read the message.

"I double-dare you to tie six balloons onto one of Professor Goodenough's trees."

My mouth dropped open.

"Tie what? Where?"

Noah repeated the dare.

I gulped. Professor Goodenough? Wasn't that the mysterious old guy who lived in the property with all the threatening signs out front?

Noah stood away from the stable door and let me through. "And if you chicken out," he said, "I'll tell everyone you're a yellow bellied, weak-kneed *wuss*."

How had I let Noah Peterson talk me into something this dumb?

By calling me a *wuss*—that's how.

Noah even said he'd come with me. Said now was a good time to go because most of the kids were out riding. Also said not to tell anyone about what we were doing because his mum would go ballistic if she found out.

Yeah. Thanks heaps, Noah. If Kate found out, she would not make me happy by sending me home—oh no— she'd throw me up on Shakespeare and make me ride till I dropped—or Shakespeare dropped—whichever came first.

After packing away the brushes and hoof-pick and curry comb and other horsy stuff I still hadn't learned the names of, I watched Noah blow up six red balloons he'd found in a cupboard full of Christmas decorations. While he huffed, I leant against the wall. While he puffed, I carefully inspected the dirt under my finger-nails. Why should I help him blow up the balloons? After all—Noah Peterson was the one who was full of hot air, not me.

Watching the red balloons bobbing and bouncing around on the floor, I shivered. What about the sign that said, 'Beware Bull-Eats People'?

Geez…what had I let Noah talk me into?

And then I decided the only way to survive the next half hour was to grab a chocolate bar, a warm sweater, and a strong dose of P.I. courage.

So, while Noah snuck a couple of bikes from the shed, I trailed inside the house. From the top drawer of the dresser in the bedroom I was sharing with Tayla and Sarah, I snaffled a Mars bar and my new red sweater—figuring if I got chomped on by the people-eating bull, at least the blood wouldn't show.

As for P.I. courage—that was a bit harder to find. Okay, my darkest pair of sunnies might help get me in the mood. And perhaps if I stashed my Bratz notebook plus my favorite silver tipped biro in the back pocket of my jodhpurs, they might come in handy.

Five minutes later, Noah and I stood at the little side track leading to the Professor's fence-line. While Noah dropped his bike on the ground and ran across to the barbwire fence, I hung back, reluctant to go any further.

"Come on, Cha!"

This wasn't like me to pass up a chance of solving a mystery. Maybe Noah was right. Maybe I was a *wuss*. I threw a nervous glance over the razor-wire fence. The threatening signs had suddenly developed a life of their own. They were glaring at me—warning me to stay on my side of the fence.

A strange silence settled over the paddock as we lay on our stomachs and prepared to wriggle under the barbed wire. A sinister silence. A silence that made the hairs on the back of my neck stand up and shiver.

"See anything?"

"Nope. All clear," whispered Noah standing up on the other side and snatching a quick look over his shoulder.

"Have you been in here before?" I asked passing the balloons over the fence to him.

"Yeah, once. But Mum found out and was so mad she wouldn't let me ride for a week."

No riding for a week? In that case perhaps this wasn't such a bad idea.

"Did you find out what the professor is hiding? Why he's surrounded by all these signs?"

"Nah. He caught me as soon as I snuck under the fence. Sent me packing and then rang Mum." Noah screwed up his nose. "He threatened to ring the police next time."

Now he tells me.

"Don't worry," my partner-in-crime added. "This won't take more than a couple of minutes. Now, hurry up and get under the wire. This isn't a picnic you know."

"Why can't we just tie the balloons to the fence line?"

"'Cos that's not what the dare said."

Who cares what the dare said.

As I followed Noah under the fence, the sleeve of my new red sweater caught on the barbed wire. Blast. Even if the Professor, or Kate, or the bull didn't kill me—Mum would. This sweater cost fifty dollars.

As soon as I stood up on the other side of the fence, Noah handed me the balloons and took off in the direction of the trees.

"Hang on! Wait for me!"

Tightening my fist on the balloon strings I scuttled after him. *I guess he's right,* I thought, as I jogged along, *this shouldn't take more than a couple of minutes and then we'll be on our bikes and heading back to the stables.*

Feeling more confident, I lengthened my stride and eyed the row of trees growing in front of the professor's rambling old house. The sooner the balloons were tied on one of their branches the better.

Half way across the paddock, a sudden movement behind the pepper trees caught my eye.

Oh, nooooooooo!

The movement had horns—and angry, red-rimmed eyes.

"Look out!" yelled Noah, his legs pumping faster. "It's the bull! Head for the nearest tree and start climbing."

As if I needed telling.

With my heart belting out a drum-roll, I galloped toward the trees at the back of the paddock. One quick glance over my shoulder told me it would be a race to the death. The bull, bellowing in fury, nostrils fanned wide, was zeroing in on my scarlet jumper and the six bright red balloons.

And his four well-muscled legs looked to be galloping a whole lot faster than my two skinny ones.

6

Perched precariously on a bendy branch six feet from the ground, I felt about as safe as a fly in a spider-web. Even if the branch didn't break and dump me under the bull's stamping feet—I'd probably lose my balance and fall and end up as mashed potato.

What a fantastic adventure. Not. I couldn't wait to tell Noah what I thought of his sucky double-dare. My throat felt full of rocks. When I opened my mouth to yell for help, all that came out was a crusty creaky croak. Both my hands were scratched and bleeding. My new red sweater was history. And I'd lost my silver biro in the mad scramble to climb the tree, so couldn't even record the important points of my soon-to-be ghastly death.

Blinking, I peered down at the tail-swishing, deadly-horned critter snorting his fury below. And caught my breath. The way the bull was eying me off, he'd evidently missed out on his breakfast this morning. I suddenly knew what it felt like to be a tempting piece of cheese waiting for a hungry mouse to pounce.

How long would it take before someone at *Treehaven*

discovered Noah and I were missing? Meal time probably. I glanced at my watch and felt like throwing up. It would be another three or four hours to *our* next meal—and if the bull had his way—only minutes to his.

Where was Noah?

I stretched my neck to see how the mastermind of this madness was getting on. Hidden in the foliage of the massive pepper tree beside me, he'd disappeared from view. Not a movement or point of color betrayed him. It was almost like he'd been beamed up by aliens—or borrowed Harry Potter's cloak of Invisibility.

Suddenly, a fearsome snort from below yanked me back to reality. The bull, his black hide sweating in the sun, had caught sight of a runaway red balloon. With a toss of his massive head he batted the balloon into the air and onto his knife-like horns. I shuddered. Tried to swallow a frog-sized lump in my throat. What if that balloon had been me? Fascinated, I watched him toss his plaything up and down until a loud bang sent a curious magpie scurrying off in fright.

"Barnaby! Heel!"

The command sliced through the air making both the bull and me turn our heads in unison.

Oh-uh!

It was the professor. He was hobbling toward us, leaning heavily on a knobbly brown stick. I peered closer, expecting to see a ferocious giant of a dog called Barnaby. Instead, the big black bull grinned a welcome at the frail old man with the long white beard. He lumbered across and put his huge head on the man's shoulder.

"Good work, Barnaby," the professor said giving the big slobbering head a pat. "Better than that useless, no-good, dozy watch-dog of mine." He looked around and bellowed. "Where are you, Pedro? If you are asleep again I will put pepper on your tail."

Down the path came a flea-sized Chihuahua looking more like a kid's wind-up toy than a vicious watch-dog. His ears were pricked, his tail stood straight and his stiff match-stick legs were burning rubber. The look on his face seemed to say, 'Who me? Sleeping? I'd rather be caught robbing a bank.'

Scooping up the tiny fawn and white dog and depositing it in one of his many voluminous coat pockets, the Professor glared up at me.

"Now," he growled, banging his walking-stick against the tree-trunk. "What are we going to do with this girl-child, Barnaby?"

Please—don't ask Barnaby. He might still be thinking of the game he played with the red balloon.

"Do you know the meaning of the words, 'No Trespassing', girl?"

"Yes sir." My voice came out all weak and wobbly. Didn't sound like my voice at all. I cleared my throat and tried again. "It was just a bit of fun. The dare-box dared me to tie six red balloons to one of your trees."

I looked across at the pepper tree. Where was *Short*

Dark and Irritating when I needed him to back me up?

Hmm…evidently turned into *Scared Pathetic and Silent.*

"Dare box?" The professor's forehead creased into paddock sized furrows.

I nodded without answering. Too complicated.

The strange old man with a bull's head resting on his shoulder and a toy guard-dog snuggled in his coat pocket looked like something from a wacky cartoon. He wore baggy pants, so old and dirty they'd probably fall to bits if he ever decided to wash them and a long button-less overcoat faded to a shabby shade of grey and done up around the middle with a hunk of green twine. His hair, silvery white and so wild, birds could have nested in there, straggled across his shoulders, while his tangled, barbwire beard finished at his waist. I could even see strands of spaghetti he'd probably spilt in his beard a month ago, still resting in the tangles, together with something green that could have been spinach, broccoli, or even moldy cheese. And what about those boots? They must have been three or four sizes too big because every step he took I could hear plopping, squelchy, thumping noises.

Was Professor Goodenough a crook? Crazy? Or just a big old pussycat?

"Are you going to climb down the tree now or stay there until the police arrive?" he asked.

A big old pussycat? Not.

I threw a glance at Barnaby who snorted and rolled his

red-rimmed eyes in evident delight at the professor's words.

"Er...I think I'll stay where I am, if that's okay with you."

"Are you on your own?"

I thought I saw a slight movement in the pepper-tree. Was Noah going to show his face and come clean at last?

"Well—"

The movement in the pepper-tree stopped. Froze. Seemed to be holding its breath.

Ha. Now we knew who was a wuss...

"Yes," I said, nodding my head slowly. "Seems like I'm all alone."

For some reason I thought of my good friend, Jack. If he'd been with me, by now, he'd probably have fallen out of the tree trying to help me, accidentally knocked the professor over and given the bull a bloody nose with his elbow.

As though his fingers didn't work very well, the Professor picked at the rope around his middle until the knot came loose. He glared up at me again.

"Right, girl. Down you come." He fashioned the rope into a loop and slipped it over Barnaby's head. "The bull won't hurt you. And what is more, you are giving me a crick in the neck with all this tedious looking up."

"But—"

"Hurry up. I have work to do. I can't waste time talking to a trespasser."

"You're sure about Barnaby?"

The Professor let his hand caress the bull's small furry ears. "Barnaby will not be a problem." He paused, his dark eyes growing darker. "Unless you try running away."

Carefully I swung my leg over the branch and slid to the ground. Up close, both Barnaby and the Professor looked larger and even more frightening.

"I-I'm sorry. L-look—"

I tried to clear my throat but it felt like a lump of cement was stuck in my windpipe. Holy catfish! What was the matter with me? I was acting like a soggy marshmallow instead of a junior P.I. Straightening my shoulders, I took a deep breath. Now was my chance to ask questions, get some answers and solve the mystery of the threatening signs.

After all…solving mysteries was what I was good at.

First, I put on my Sunday-best, good-girl face and dredged up my most polite and contrite voice.

"I'm really sorry about trespassing, Professor. Truly I am. You see, someone dared me to tie the balloons to one of your trees."

Then I changed my face to a serious, let's-get-some-answers-going-here sort of expression.

"Now, tell me," I said, looking him up and down and wondering again about the green stuff in his beard. "Why do you have all these 'No Trespassing' signs on your property? What are you trying to hide?"

Ignoring my questions, the professor leaned on his stick

and turned in the direction of the house. "Follow me, girl. You can wait on the porch while I contact your parents."

Contact my parents? On their honeymoon?

Geez. I could imagine how happy *that* would make them. Not. Perhaps, I decided, as I trudged along behind the Professor, I should stop practicing my private investigator skills and dig up some cool, Chiana Ryan charm instead.

But how? I didn't *do* charm. That was Tayla's specialty. Me—I rubbed people up the wrong way. If I smiled and batted my eyelashes at the professor, the way Tayla did— he'd scowl, then completely ignore me. If I told him how intelligent he was—he'd scowl, then completely ignore me. If I told him I thought he was a crook—he'd scowl—

It was about then I noticed a baby crocodile running across the professor's foot.

"That's a—that's a—" I spluttered, running backwards until my body crashed against a tree-trunk.

"Oh! Botheration and damn."

As the tiny leathery creature hissed at a curious Barnaby, the professor tut-tutted impatiently. He dug deep into his coat pocket, pulled out a sleepy, blinking Pedro and set him on the ground.

"Guard the girl," he ordered, then bent forward and caught the hissing reptile by the back of the neck.

"You! Stay!" he growled, pointing a finger at me like I was a dog and he expected me to sit or roll over. "I will be back in a minute."

With the baby crocodile still spitting at him, the Professor limped off toward a tumble-down shed built onto the side of the house.

Hmmm…interesting.

Could whatever was hidden inside that shed be the reason for all the 'No Trespassing' signs?

I took a hesitant step forward.

Pedro skipped across in front of me and barred his teeth apologetically.

Guard the girl.

"Hi little fellow. Aren't you cute?"

I knelt down on one knee and tickled the Chihuahua behind the ears. The little dog rolled over on his back, kicked his legs and dribbled dreamily, while I rubbed his stomach. When I stood up he began jumping up and down on my leg like a tennis ball, yapping in delight.

Now for the bull.

In my pocket was a carrot. Kate had told me to give it to Shakespeare when I'd finished brushing him but what with Noah and his stupid double-dare, I'd completely forgotten about it.

Until now.

"Here you go, Barnaby, old buddy."

Eyes closed, face screwed up in anticipation of losing several fingers, I held the carrot out on the flat of my hand. Please…*please* let the bull prefer carrots to fingers.

As I felt his warm, leathery sandpapery tongue tickle the palm of my hand, I held my breath. Finally, running out of air, I opened my eyes and checked my hand. Yep! All five fingers still attached and wriggling.

"Good boy, Barnaby."

He'd not only eaten the carrot but if his goofy face was anything to go by he'd enjoyed the treat.

Now…should I escape or check out the shed?

I knew I should escape while the Professor was busy. Sneak down the path, find my bike, high-tail it back to the stables and get Kate to come back and rescue Noah. But how could I leave without first taking a peek in the shed? My P.I. instincts insisted I find out what the professor was up to.

One eye on Barnaby, I tiptoed past the trees then ran softly in the direction of the rusty galvanized iron shed. Why did the professor object to trespassers sniffing around his property? Was the shed full of illegal crocodiles? Escaped convicts? Dead bodies?

I pressed my nose against the dirty window pane. This was it. Once again, Chiana Ryan, famous junior P.I. was about to solve a baffling and complicated mystery.

At first, I couldn't see a thing through the dirt-streaked window. And then I blinked in disbelief. The professor's shed hid no dead bodies—no escaped convicts—no snapping, snarling crocodiles…

Instead…the professor's shed was full of eggs.

7

Eggs.

There must have been at least a hundred of them inside the professor's tumble-down shed.

Big eggs, little eggs, white eggs, blue eggs, spotted eggs. All resting in boxes or baskets filled with straw. All with heat-lamps keeping them warm and snug. I squashed my nose hard against the dirty glass window. Was that a crack in one of the eggs? Was the egg nearest the window breaking open?

Yesssss!

Whatever was inside was about to hatch. I held my breath. Felt my heart quicken. And then it happened. Part of the shell fell away and out popped something small, jellybean pink and with dark bulges where the eyes should be. This was no fluffy baby chicken. So what was it? Was the professor hatching some alien species from another planet?

Just then, the professor shuffled from a room at the back of the shed, shaking his head. I could hear what sounded like muffled squawks and cheeps from behind the door as he closed it behind him. Then he straightened his bent shoulders, lifted his drooping head and looked around the shed. His eyes lit up and he ka-thumped across the cement floor toward the broken egg, his wooden walking-stick tap-tapping in his hurry.

"Oh how sweet," he cooed, a warm smile lighting up his wrinkled old face as he gazed down at the ugly pink baby. "Your mother isn't around, my darling, but Uncle Tad will look after you."

Uncle Tad?

He looked up and his eyes met mine through the murky glass.

Immediately he changed from sweet caring *Uncle Tad* back into the steely-eyed stern professor who set his two-ton bull on anyone foolish enough to ignore the 'No Trespassing' signs on his property.

Time to split.

Little Pedro had become my best friend but there was no way Barnaby would let me escape without a chase.

A chase I had as much chance of winning as the lottery.

But what if I wasn't on foot?

The professor had parked his battered ute only meters from the shed door. I glanced through the car window. There were the keys—just begging to be used. My heart hammered against my chest as I tugged on the door-handle. The car wasn't locked. If I drove to the front gate, jumped out and wriggled under the barbwire—there was a chance I'd beat the bull.

But could I drive a car? I'd seen my mum behind the wheel, working the gear stick and the foot pedals. It looked easy enough. Scooping Pedro up under my arm in case he accidentally got under the car wheels, I wrenched the door open and threw myself on the seat.

Pedro snuggled up beside me and went to sleep. Barnaby bunted the car door with his horns and bellowed at me. The professor burst through the shed door waving his stick and hollering, "Come back here, girl-child!"

As if.

Heart still thumping madly I turned the key in the keyhole thingy and held my breath. From under the bonnet of the car came this loud growling noise like a vacuum cleaner with a bad case of the flu. Okay—we had lift-off. Stretching my legs forward at full-stretch I pushed down on one of the pedals and crunched the gear stick. The ute back-fired like an explosive fart, bunny-hopped forward, then took off straight toward the shed. My breath got stuck somewhere between my lungs and my throat. Barnaby and the professor stood frozen to the spot, their eyes bigger and rounder than prize-winning pumpkins.

Hands fisted around the ancient leather on the steering-wheel I yanked hard left and heard a rasping crunch. Oh! Oh! I bit my bottom lip and hung on to the wheel. The car had missed the professor and the bull, scraped the corner of the shed and was bucketing along the track.

"Noah," I yelled, slamming my foot on the brake when I reached the big pepper tree. "You have two seconds to get out of that tree and into the car. Or I go without you."

Through the rear-vision mirror I could see Barnaby and the professor. The professor was shuffling awfully fast for an old guy on a stick and the bull looked angry enough to eat tin cans.

Out of the tree like a bag of spuds, dropped *Short Dark and Irritating*.

"You don't know how to drive!" he accused glaring at me as if I'd kidnapped the Pope.

No *sorry*. No *thanks*. No *great stuff, Cha*. Just a typical boy-remark. I wanted to stuff him in a rubbish bin and jam the lid on tight.

"Get in or get gored," I snapped, taking my foot off the brake and lurching forward again in two giant bunny-hops.

"Hang on!" Noah shouted, his voice cracking in his hurry. He flung himself into the car and sprawled face-first on the seat beside me.

"Look out for the dog!"

"Oooowch!"

Too late…

I ignored Noah's painful howl and glanced over my shoulder. Barnaby was only two car lengths away.

"Get ready to run!"

"That rotten dog bit me."

"I would too if you landed on top of me. Poor Pedro. I bet you tasted disgusting."

Bouncing in and out of the deep holes in the driveway

was like clinging to a rowboat in stormy seas. I screeched to a halt at the gate, threw Pedro a last kiss, then dived head first out the car door and hit the ground rolling.

And I kept rolling—right under the barbed wire fence.

My breath chugging in my throat, I sat up and shook my head. Whew…I'd made it! But what about Noah?

Another yell shattered the air. Uh! Oh! I looked up just in time to see Barnaby's horns graze the seat of Noah's pants as he scrabbled and clawed his way under the rolls of barbed wire.

"Come on, Noah," I said, smothering a giggle as I stood up and dragged my bike out of the dirt. "Stop playing games."

"Ha. Ha." Noah glared at me before clambering on his bike. "Tell anyone about what just happened and you're history."

We biked in silence for a couple of minutes. No way could I confide in Noah about the eggs. He'd blab for sure. And somehow I knew it was important to keep what I'd discovered in the professor's shed a secret. Okay, Professor Goodenough was scary-looking and really weird, but the expression on his face when he saw the egg hatching showed another side to the man. A softer side. It reminded me of my mum when she spotted Mrs. Teagle's new baby from down the street. All gooey and smiley and honey-sweet. Sort of sick, actually.

But what animal baby is jelly-bean pink with no eyes?

"And don't tell mum about us going to the Professor's

place." It was Noah, breaking into my thoughts again as we cycled up the driveway to *Treehaven*.

I shook my head in disbelief.

As if.

"'Cos if you do—I can make things real ugly for you here."

"Whatever."

Geez…under which rock did Kate find this creep? No wonder Sarah was a pain in butt. Must run in the family.

"I mean it!"

"I know you do, Noah. What else would I expect from a cowardly creep?"

"Take that back!"

"Why should I? You didn't even show your face when the professor found me up the tree."

"So? You were the one doing the double dare—not me."

"In case you've forgotten, the stupid double dare was your stupid idea."

By the time we reached the bike-shed I felt like hurling the bike at Noah's head. Instead, I gritted my teeth and gave him one of my frostiest glares. Noah Peterson wasn't worth getting all sweaty about. And anyway, real P.I.'s didn't lose their cool.

"Stop right there!" It was Kate and by the way her lips pressed together in a thin straight line and her eyes narrowed to slits—she wasn't happy to see us.

"I've just got off the phone from speaking to Professor Goodenough."

Uh! Oh!

Busted.

"He tells me two of my pupils trespassed on his property, upset his bull and almost wrecked his car."

"How did he—" I began.

"Jodhpurs," she responded.

Noah scowled at me. "If you hadn't made me get in the car, old fossil-face wouldn't have known I was there."

"Made you?" I spluttered wishing I still had the bike in my hands. "Why you—"

"Enough!" roared Kate. "Inside. Both of you! We'll discuss this after dinner. Meanwhile, there's twenty pounds of potatoes waiting to be peeled in the kitchen. And I don't want to hear any complaints from Mrs. Brown about either of you slacking off until the job's finished."

My mouth dropped somewhere down near my new riding boots.

Twenty pounds of potatoes?

I was tired. I was dirty. My hands were bleeding. And all I wanted to do was get as far away from *Short Dark and Irritating* as possible—preferably by sending him to another country—or better yet—another planet.

I sighed and followed Kate inside. A cold kitchen. A sharp knife. Twenty pounds of potatoes to peel. And a constantly whining Noah.

Not a good combination.

8

By the time I logged onto the computer in the Games Room an hour later, my fingers felt like they'd been run over by a tractor. *Geez.* I never knew peeling potatoes was such a complicated art-form. According to Mrs. Brown, the cook, potato peel an inch thick was waste and washing a potato and leaving the skin on was as bad as wearing muddy boots to a wedding. Perhaps she should start an elite Potato Peeling Course at the local high school!

I uploaded my Gmail address on Google and there, in my inbox, was an email from Jack. Yay! With Tayla dribbling horse-talk non-stop I couldn't get any sense from her. Sarah, as usual, was too wrapped up in Sarah to be of use to anyone but Sarah. So…I couldn't wait to bounce ideas off my only sane P.I. assistant, Jack.

Like—why was the professor's shed full of eggs when there wasn't a chicken in sight?

From: *Jackolantern@optusnet.com.au*
To: *Chianaryan@gmail.com*
Subject: EGGY BUSINESS
Hi Cha,

After we win the footy-match on Saturday (yep, it's in the bag) Dad said he'd drive me straight to Treehaven. Is there a black stallion waiting 4 me there? I always fancied myself on a black stallion, called Devil.

Yesterday I sprung Leroy from the boarding-kennel 4 a day so we could snoop around the museum. While I grilled a couple of witnesses, Leroy searched 4 clues. He sniffed the front door, a wooden chair and the receptionist's leg. We didn't learn much. Seems like that museum curator who bumped into you, you know the one with the garlicky breath and greasy hair, wasn't a curator at all. I described him to the receptionist and she just shook her head. Said no-one on the staff looked like that.

BTW Leroy sends his love and says to tell you he hates being on a diet and could he have at least half a Tim Tam a day.

Gotta go. It's our last footy-training B4 the big match and Dingo and Salmon are waiting for me in the kitchen. If I don't go now there'll be no food left in the fridge.

C U Saturday.

Your two brilliant P.I. assistants,

Jack and Leroy.

I grinned, picturing my 'two brilliant P.I. assistants' working together on the 'Case of the Missing Dinosaur-egg'. This was way weird. I'd left an egg-mystery at home only to discover a new and totally baffling egg-mystery right up the road from the riding-school.

Just as I hit the reply button to answer Jack's email,

Sarah poked her head around the doorway. Naturally she was the bearer of bad news.

"Hey, Cha, Aunt Kate wants to see you in her office and she looks real snotty. You'd better not keep her waiting."

What did I tell you?

Sarah clomped across the room and stood beside me. "You're totally weird, Cha."

Ready to bite her head off and feed it to the chooks, I looked up, opened my mouth to give her a blast, then shut it again. Strange. My step-sister wasn't smirking. Or laughing. Or giving me her cat's behind *I told you so* face.

"So," she said. "What mess are you in now?"

What did she care?

"Nothing much."

She glanced at Jack's email. "More trouble?"

"Nothing you'd be interested in."

Sarah's face went from sugar to lemons. She gave an *okay-don't-tell-me-then* shrug and mumbled, "Thought things were different now," sniffed loudly, and stormed off.

I jumped to my feet.

"Sarah, come back. I'm sorry," I called out, but by the time I'd reached the door she was nowhere in sight.

Sheesh…how could I ever work that girl out? One minute she acted like I had chicken-pox—next she was getting all huffy because I wasn't confiding in her.

Throwing myself down at the computer again, I sighed. And on top of that Kate was waiting to chew me out. I may as well be spending my holidays at some crappy military-school. Perhaps when Jack arrived on Saturday we'd start having fun. Perhaps I could even get him to challenge *Short Dark and Irritating* to an arm-wrestling contest.

Loser (Noah) gets buried in the manure pit.

From: *Chianaryan@gmail.com*

To: *Jackolantern@optusnet.com.au*

Subject: EGGY BUSINESS

Hi Jack,

Will you hurry up and win that footy-game? I need a brilliant P.I. assistant desperately. You're not going to believe this but today I stumbled across another egg-mystery. Tell you about it when you get here.

Just one question: What's got pink skin, no fur and dark lumps for eyes? No. It's not a riddle. About an hour ago I saw it hatching out of an egg. Not getting much help from Tayla or Sarah, so pack your magnifying glass, trench-coat and notebook. I need you.

This is secret stuff. I'm deleting this message as soon as I send it. Advise you to do the same at your end.

Chiana Ryan (P.I. Extraordinaire)

p.s. Tell Leroy I've saved some black jelly-beans for him as a special treat when I get home.

I watched Jack's email go off into cyber-space, then shut down the computer, stood up and let out a sigh. The sigh ended way down deep in the heels of my socks. It was time to face the lioness in her den.

I glanced down at my scruffy, tree-climbing, barbed-wire-fighting clothes. No time to change, so I quickly ripped the ruined jumper off over my head and scrubbed at the dirt and grass stains on my jodhpurs with a glob of spit. Using the computer screen as a mirror, I checked my reflection. A witch looked back at me. Why hadn't Sarah told me I had half a gum tree stuck in my hair?

Three minutes later I knocked on the door of Kick-ass Kate's office.

"Enter."

Enter? Geez… this was as bad as going to the Principal's office at school.

I turned the handle and inched open the door. Come on, I argued with myself, this is only Sarah's Aunt Kate. She's not a scary Dementor from a Harry Potter movie— waiting to suck the life-force from me as soon as I walked into the room. What was the worst Kate could do? Send me home to an empty house? Make me ride twenty horses a day?

Ride twenty horses a day? I almost threw up all over her pale green carpet at such a terrifying thought.

"Sit down please, Chiana."

My shaky legs were happy to slump onto a comfortable brown sofa next to a wall covered in framed photos. Awesome photos of a much younger Kate riding the most beautiful dappled grey horse I'd ever seen. They were flying over jumps the size of large buildings.

"I have something to show you," said Kate.

"You do?" My voice came out as a squeak. I cleared my

throat and looked down at the boot-shaped mud pattern I'd left on her pale green floor.

Kate handed me a box. "I thought you might find this interesting. I found it under Noah's bed."

If she thought a box under her kid's bed was interesting, what would she think of the fake handcuffs, fake blood and fake beard under mine?

"See what it is?"

It was an old cardboard box. The same old cardboard box Noah had shoved under my nose in Shakespeare's stable. The same old cardboard box I'd been tricked into taking a double dare from. I blinked up at Kate, confused. What did she want me to do? Pick another dare? Praise Noah's scratchy handwriting? Place the box over my head?

"Why don't you take a look at the other dares inside the box?"

I dipped my hand in the box and pulled out a piece of screwed up paper. After flattening it out I read, "I double-dare you to tie six red balloons to one of Professor Goodenough's trees."

What?

"Try another one," suggested Kate, sitting on the top of her desk and giving me a conspirator's smirk.

I grabbed another piece of screwed up paper. "I double-dare you to tie six red balloons to one of Professor Goodenough's trees."

I grabbed another…and another…and another.

All the same!

"Why that—"

"Yep," broke in Kate. "You were set up by a rat passing himself off as a boy."

"That creep!"

"I agree."

"A total piece of dog's poop."

Kate stood up. "My darling son is outside cleaning stables. After that he'll be cleaning toilets, saddles, the manure heap, the pigeon loft, the goats' shed and the pig pens. He's also been banned from riding for a week. Instead, it's *his* job to teach *you* to ride. In fact, if you're not riding well enough to compete in our Cross-Country event on the last day of your holiday, Noah's riding ban will continue for a month. That means he'll miss the Junior Show jumping Championships, an event he's been training for since he won the finals last year."

Wow! And I thought *my* mother was an alien!

I checked Kate's eyes to see if they were spinning around in her head—all clear—so I grinned and stood up, ready to leave.

The sight of Noah cleaning toilets was too good a show to miss.

9

Tayla sat cross-legged on the tack room floor. Her two-toned jodhpurs and yellow polo shirt looked like they'd just been removed from a store window. How did she do it? She could have been a model on a catwalk instead of a girl who'd been riding a hot sweaty horse less than fifteen minutes ago. Not even a smudge of dirt on her nose. *Geez. I only had to look at a horse and I ended up with thick grey dribble all down the front of my shirt.*

It was late Saturday afternoon. Jack's team had won the footy finals and as soon as his father had driven him to *Treehaven*, I'd called a secret meeting—in the tack room—with the door closed. And a sign out front saying, 'If you enter—prepare to die!'

The meeting wasn't going well. I'd been yakking on for the last ten minutes, reading from my notes, explaining to the others about the professor, the bull and Pedro the Chihuahua and how I'd watched an egg hatch.

At last Tayla crinkled her nose in disbelief. "It couldn't be a platypus, Cha. That's too totally freaky to make sense."

"Okay…what other creature is born with jellybean pink skin and looks like this?" I showed her a picture of a baby platypus in the book I'd borrowed from the Gawler public library that morning.

Sarah, her knees up round her chin, her suede boots arranged beside her, sat painting ten perfectly shaped toenails a glaringly hideous shade of *Vomit Orange*.

"Admit it, Cha," she said her eyes never leaving her toes. "You made a mistake. After all, you said yourself the window was streaked with dirt. What you saw hatching was probably a baby chicken or a duckling. They're both small and with wet feathers could look sort of pink."

"But what if I didn't make a mistake? We have to find out for sure."

"No we don't," bleated Tayla nervously. "That crazy professor guy gives me the creeps. I'll have nightmares tonight just thinking about his scary bull."

Sarah shook her head. "It's too risky, Cha. If we get caught, Aunt Kate will not only hit the roof, she'll bring it down around our ears. And for what? Something you *thought* you saw through a dirty window."

I sighed. Glanced around at the saddles, bridles and pieces of leather I couldn't put a name to. Breathed in the smell of sweaty horse and stale manure. This new mystery seemed to be going down the toilet before it even started. But I couldn't give up. No mystery to solve meant I had no story to write.

Scowling at Sarah and Tayla, I pulled my notebook

from my pocket.

"Okay, here's what we do," I declared, chewing on the end of one of my favorite pink biros. "If what I saw wasn't a platypus it might have been some alien species. So…we wait until the professor is out then we sneak in and check the eggs in his shed. See what's *really* being hatched in there."

Tayla hurled a damp saddle-cleaning sponge at my head. "Didn't you hear a word I said? I am *not* going onto that scary guy's property. Not even to rescue a baby platypus."

"Which actually is a wet chicken," added Sarah, finishing off her nails and screwing the lid back on the bottle.

I sighed again. Since I'd arrived at *Treehaven* that's all I seemed to be doing. What was wrong with my P.I. assistants? Had they all gone soft on me?

"Hang on a minute," said Jack, leaping to his feet and knocking down a large tin of horse-vitamins with his elbow. "What if the professor is an egg-thief? What if he was responsible for the theft of the dinosaur egg at the museum? What if we found the dinosaur egg in his shed?"

"Wow!" I caught the glimmer of excitement in Jack's eyes and grinned at him. "I hadn't thought of that."

Sarah sniffed. "Yeah. And what if the world is really flat?"

Ignoring Sarah's put-down, I felt an electric buzz start in my fingertips, race up both arms then skip in a tingling rush through the rest of my body. Hey, Jack could be onto something big here.

"What if Professor Goodenough is an egg smuggler?" he continued, his freckles dancing across his nose.

"Or even a mad scientist who's experimenting with animals," I added.

"What if he's trying to clone a dinosaur by using the DNA of the fossilized egg?"

"Double wow!"

"Do you two know how crazy you sound?" Sarah coolly slipped the bottle of *Vomit Orange* into her jodhpurs' pocket, picked up her suede riding-boots and stood up. "You saw a chicken hatching from an egg and now you've decided it's a scene from Jurassic Park."

Her comment was like a bucket of ice water over the head. Sarah was right. Jack and I were being ridiculous. I rammed my notebook back into my pocket and felt a blush creep up my neck and spread across my cheeks. Grrrrrrrr! Anyone want a step-sister for free?

Evidently satisfied with the way she'd broken up our meeting, Princess Sarah strolled to the tack room door on her newly painted feet.

"I'm off," she said in her I'm-so-cool voice. "Unless you uncover a *real* mystery—count me out. I don't want to be grounded like Noah. I came here to ride and that's what I'm going to do."

I watched Tayla get to her feet too. Gracefully, like one of those long-legged dancers from the ballet Mum had taken me to see for my twelfth birthday. I could tell Tayla agreed with Sarah because her eyes looked like Leroy's when he'd been caught fossicking in the rubbish-bin.

"Sorry, Cha," she said sheepishly. "I love riding Angel and I'd just die if Kate grounded me."

Geez…what was it with Tayla and Sarah? How was I supposed to solve our latest mystery when two of my assistants had been so badly bitten by the horse-bug they'd turned into marshmallows?

I lifted an eye-brow in the direction of my last hope. "Jack?"

"I'm in."

Tayla fidgeted with the end of one shiny blonde curl. "Cha, if you keep on with this egg mystery stuff—be careful. Don't let Noah find out or he'll tell his mum just to get back at you. He's spewing 'cos he's not allowed to ride and blames you for everything."

Sarah's head popped back around the doorway and caught the end of Tayla's warning. She grinned her sly tiger-grin at me. "Talking about my sweet lovable cousin, you'd better hide, Cha. He's mad as—"

Noah came crashing into the tack-room, his face set in a screwed-up scowl.

"Hey, you!" he yelled. "How am I supposed to teach you to ride if you don't even show up for your lessons?"

I gave Jack a mock-frown. "Do you think he means me?"

"You? Nah. Wouldn't talk to *you* like that. He must be

talking to the wall."

Noah's scowl deepened. "Ha. Ha. The joke's on you, 'cos I'd rather *teach* the wall. Get your riding helmet on Chiana and let's go."

That morning Noah had made me ride bareback. That's right…no saddle. He'd lunged me on Shakespeare for half an hour of bone-grating, stomach-jolting, butt-banging torture. If you've ever bounced around on a horse with a backbone so hard, so sharp your rear feels like it's on fire— you'll know what I mean. If you haven't—don't go there.

"Sorry Noah, I'm too tired. I'll see how I feel tomorrow."

"Ooh no you don't." His scowl turned into a dragon-snarl as he stepped closer. "*Wuss!*"

Noah was at it again. Calling me a *wuss*. If only Jack didn't have a death-grip on my arm I'd stick my fingers down Noah's throat, yank out his tongue and feed it to the stable cat.

"Mum says you have to ride in our Cross-country event next week," Noah went on, his teeth clenched so tightly I half expected a couple to snap off. "So I'm going to make sure you're ready for that—even if it kills you!"

Of course. Noah couldn't compete in the Junior Show jumping Championships if he didn't have me riding well by the end of next week. I squinted, screwed up my nose and stuck out my tongue.

"Okay," I said pushing myself off the pile of horse rugs and standing on legs that felt like mushy oatmeal.

His words, '*even if it kills you*' echoed around in my head. If this afternoon's lesson was half as bad as this morning's I wanted the theme song from 'Titanic' to be played at my funeral.

Even if I survived, I thought, as I followed *Short Dark and Irritating* outside, I'd be sitting on a feather-cushion. Too tired to eat. Too tired to talk. And too tired to think about the new egg mystery.

I bet no other private investigator in the whole universe was ever made to ride a horse without a saddle in the middle of solving a mystery.

10

With only five days to C day (Cross-Country day), it hurt to sit on a wooden chair or use my legs for anything other than holding up my body. Three lessons a day, two with Noah and a group lesson with Kate, also meant I couldn't get the smell of horse from my skin, my hair, my clothes, my mouth and even my eyelashes.

After finishing our group lesson for the day, Kate decided it was time to build the Cross-Country course. She gave Jack and me the job of building jumps along the fence-line next to Professor Goodenough's property.

Which of course led to Jack and I discussing the egg-mystery.

"We can't just break into the shed. That's against the law," I protested when Jack suggested we sneak out at night dressed all in black and try the keys from his 'special' key-ring to open the shed door.

Jack had been collecting different shaped keys from the age of six and now owned close to two hundred.

"Well, how else can we find out what the professor's up to?"

I shook my head. "We need a workable plan."

"What you got in mind?"

"It's a bit complicated. If we wait until the professor goes out then sneak in—that's trespassing. If we ring and ask his permission—he'll tell us to get lost."

We trudged along the path in silence for several more minutes. Me, pushing a rusty wheelbarrow full of paint tins, brushes, hammers, nails, buckets, a shovel and a broken toolbox. Jack, humping an elephant sized backpack.

"What if we dress up as meter-readers?" I suggested.

I could picture myself in an official meter-reading coat, a grey wig and coke-bottle glasses. To make the picture complete I'd carry a clipboard in one hand and a mobile phone in the other.

"And do what?"

"Well, while you distract the professor by explaining how he could cut down on his electricity bill, I could see if the shed was unlocked."

Jack's cheeky grin set his freckles dancing. "Or what about pretending to be the Avon Lady? You could keep the Prof. at the door by selling him wrinkle cream, while I did the Sherlock Holmes bit in the shed."

I shook my head. "Sherlock Holmes smokes a pipe. One puff and you'd choke."

We rounded the corner and came to the site of the first of the jumps along the fence-line. "This must be the hole Noah dug yesterday," I said, smirking at the thought of

Noah getting all hot and sweaty for a change. "Kate wants us to fill the hole with water."

"I'll do that," offered Jack tossing the back-pack on the ground and hunting in the wheelbarrow. "Kate says horses hate jumping into water." He pulled a face. "So I guess this is where most of us will fall off."

The newly dug pit was about fifty centimeters deep, ten meters long and lined with blue plastic to stop the water from soaking into the ground. In front of the pit Noah had rolled a largish log. The idea was to jump the log into the water and trot out the other side. I shuddered at the thought. I could see myself falling off over the log and sitting in the water—wet, muddy and horseless. That's if I made it this far.

"I'll go look for a tap while you wire the jump number to the log." Jack unfastened the straps on his back-pack and drew out a white square with a bright red number eight painted across the middle. I took the number then handed Jack two plastic buckets from the wheel-barrow.

Jack wandered off while I stared at the professor's fence, high chain wire, topped with three strands of barbed wire. This was totally weird. No-one built a fence like this unless they had something to hide.

Unable to make sense of the professor's eggs or his fence, I knelt in the dirt beside the log and started work. The wire was thick and awkward. It cut into my fingers as I threaded it through the hole on top of the number then tried bending it around the log.

Gloves. I needed gloves to twist the wire. I stuck my hand in the wheelbarrow and hunted through the gear. No gloves. It was as I sucked blood from my sore finger and thought—hey, I might wait until Jack comes back, let him twist the stupid wire—that I heard the noise. A sort of faint whimpering sound. At first I thought it must be a bird but when the whimper changed to a bark, then a yelp, I scrambled to my feet. It was a dog. But where was the sound coming from?

"Hey, Cha! Come here! Quick!"

"What is it, Jack?" I raced across to where I could see Jack kneeling on the ground.

Beside him a small furry animal snarled and struggled to get free from the fence. It was caught in the wire.

"He won't let me touch him," complained Jack. Blood dripped from his hand onto his shirt. "Every time I try to untangle his leg from the wire, he bites me."

I moved closer and gasped in surprise. "It's Pedro! Oooh, what happened, darling?"

"Who in the name of Zorro is Pedro?"

"It's the professor's guard-dog," I answered, kneeling down to stroke the little Chihuahua's head. "Quick, go get the wire-cutters from the wheelbarrow. Every time he struggles the wire digs deeper into his leg. And look—it's bleeding."

"So's my hand," muttered Jack.

While Jack went off to get the wire-cutters, I tried to calm Pedro. I told him he was a big brave dog, the wire was a nasty wicked monster, and I'd give him one of Leroy's black jelly beans if he was a good boy. His eyes, wide with fear and pain, never left my face. His whimpers grew louder. If he could speak human I'm sure he'd be saying, 'It hurts, Cha—please help me.'

"Hang on big guy," I sniffed, as his long raspy tongue licked its way up my hand. "We'll have you out in no time."

The wire from the fence had wrapped itself around the dog's back leg and I guess the more he pulled, the tighter the wire pulled back.

"Ooh…be careful, Jack," I said when he returned with the wire-cutters and knelt down ready to cut the wire. I couldn't watch. With one hand over Pedro's eyes and the other holding the dog still, I sucked in a deep breath and turned my head away.

"Okay, you can both look now."

"Thanks, Jack." With Pedro's hot smothering kisses making it hard to see what I was doing, I gently unwound the piece of wire from his leg. "There you go, boy. All free now." I scooped the little dog up and tucked him under one arm. "Now, let's take you home."

Then it hit me.

"Hey, Jack. We *do* have a plan."

"Yeah." He grinned. "We just walk up to the professor's door and knock."

"Check."

"And it's not like we'll be trespassing."

"Check."

"Because we have a good reason for being on the professor's property."

"Check again."

Jack scrambled to his feet and grinned like a three-year-old at a birthday party.

"And do you know the best part of this plan?"

I shook my head.

"I don't even have to smoke a pipe!"

11

I snuggled the little dog closer to my chest. "Okay, Pedro, let's go see if *Uncle Tad* can fix your leg."

Jack and I wriggled under the razor-sharp fence at the front of the property, brushed off the dirt and marched up the path toward the professor's front door.

All long legs and clumping boots, Jack was striding along in front of me, when suddenly he stopped. He turned around, his eyes wide, his mouth slack. When he spoke, his voice was all croaky and breathless.

"Wh-what about the b-bull?"

Like a magician pulling a rabbit from a hat, I produced two carrots from my pocket. "Da Da!" I grinned. "Don't worry, Jack. I grabbed these carrots for us to munch on while we were building the jumps. If Barnaby shows up, I guess you won't mind giving him you carrot."

Jack whooshed out his breath in relief. "Barnaby's welcome to mine. I hate carrots. They taste like orange dirt."

Tired from his fight with the fence, Pedro lay quietly in my arms, his black eyes blinking owlishly up at me.

It was about then I spotted the professor's two-ton guard-bull. He was trotting toward us, snorting, tossing his head, springing from hoof to hoof. And he looked even bigger than the last time I'd met him

Jack and I froze.

Who did I think I was? I must be going soft in the head. Why did I think a couple of carrots would stop Barnaby from killing us and tossing bits of our bodies all over the paddock, like confetti?

Pedro lifted his head and whined. He'd seen Barnaby too.

Please be telling your big mate we're friends, I prayed. *And please, God, don't let me wet my pants.*

The bull trotted closer. A few inches from becoming mincemeat, I jerked my arms out in front of me and showed Pedro to Barnaby. "L-look, Barnaby, it's your mate, Pedro! He's been hurt. We're taking him to your boss. Okay?"

Immediately Barnaby's eyes went soft. He nuzzled Pedro gently. Pedro yapped and whined in reply. Still shaking, I tucked the little dog under my arm and held out a carrot.

"Yum! Yum! Carrots, Barnaby."

At the first bite the bull looked like a little kid being fed his first chocolate Easter-egg. All gooey eyed and slobbery. I dropped the two carrots on the ground and whispered to Jack, "Let's go!"

Although we wanted to bolt, we walked like a couple of

robots toward the front door of the house, forcing ourselves not to look back. One important thing I'd learned about Barnaby was that he loved to chase things. Balloons—floating leaves—trespassers.

On the way to the house, Jack and I had to pass the professor's egg shed. The door was wide open. We stopped and looked at each other. Surely that was a sign—an invitation to go inside.

"Do you think we should see if the professor's in here?" I asked, raising my eyebrows.

"You bet."

Pretending to be Rebecca Turnbull, the fictional P.I. character in my short stories, I slid around the door frame, scuttled inside and flattened my body against the wall. My trusty assistant followed.

When Jack caught sight of all the eggs his eyes widened.

"Where's the baby platypus?" he whispered.

I shrugged and shook my head.

The door to the back room was slightly open which meant the professor was either getting very slack or he was in there.

I caught Jack's eye and pointed.

On tiptoe, with Pedro settled into the crook of one arm, I inched across the cement floor. Then, almost at the door I stopped and frowned. What if we found a body in the back room? What if the body was stiff and covered in blood?

My breath caught in my throat. My heart skittered like

possums in a tree. I needed to 'go' badly.

Perhaps we should just sneak back out again and leave Pedro at the professor's front door. As Kate wisely said, 'What the professor is doing on his own property is no business of ours.'

My mind on dead bodies and mad professors, I let out a loud and breathy *Oomph* as Jack's hard-as-cement head punched me between the shoulder blades and sent me flying. Geez. How could anyone trip over fresh air? If Jack wanted to continue as my star-assistant he'd have to learn to pick up his feet.

In an effort to save Pedro from more pain, I flung out my one free hand and connected with the wooden door in front of me. The resulting noise echoed through the shed as the wooden door crashed open, bounced against the wall, shuddered and juddered several times and then came to a stop.

In the silence that followed I poked my head around the doorway. The professor sat on the floor, blinking like a startled rabbit, legs stretched out in front of him. He'd been feeding a featherless baby cockatoo with what looked like porridge. A baby crocodile had crawled up onto his shoulder and three tiny pink jellybean-like creatures were cuddled together on a hot water bottle, asleep in his hat.

"Er…h-hello," I stammered, grinning nervously.

The professor frowned, the wrinkles on his forehead gouging into deep furrows.

"Not *you* again!" he growled.

"Um—sorry to scare you, Professor, but Jack and I found Pedro caught in the fence. It looks like he's hurt one of his back legs." I smiled at the little dog in my arms. Two sad doleful eyes blinked back up at me. "He's in pain."

"Pedro? Hurt?" The professor dropped the bowl of porridge on the floor beside the baby cockatoo and grabbed his walking stick. "Time out," he told the bird then pushed himself upright. As he hobbled toward me I noticed the tiny leathery reptile on his shoulder adjust itself more securely.

"Pedro?" The end of the dog's skinny tail wagged piteously. "You were supposed to be guarding the shed door. What were you thinking—leaving your post and trying to dig under the fence?"

Pedro closed his eyes and snuggled deeper into the soft folds of my plaid shirt.

"Perhaps he heard something?" I suggested. "There's been lots happening in the paddock next door. We're setting up a Cross-Country course in there."

"Put Pedro on the table," ordered the professor pointing to a shiny steel examination table just like the one you see in a vet's surgery.

At first I'd been too worried about the professor being angry to check my surroundings. Now, I gazed around the room and felt a shiver skitter up my spine. Had we stumbled into Dr. Jekyll's lab?

The back room behind the shed seemed to be set up like a laboratory. Expensive equipment that I didn't know the name of covered tables and shelves. The only thing I recognized was a large state-of-the-art microscope which the professor had set up on a table by the window. Was he into germs? DNA? Cloning?

Beside the microscope I could see lots of see-through test tubes containing a mysterious red chemical…

Or was it blood?

With a gulp, I clutched Pedro closer and shivered again. Cages lined every wall of the room. Cages with living creatures that squeaked, cheeped, slithered, or squawked. This egg mystery was getting curiouser and curiouser.

And scarier and scarier.

As I lay Pedro gently on the cold table I tried to stop my hands from shaking. For a moment it felt like a scene from a horror movie. You know, just before the two innocent victims are captured, tortured and hacked into tiny pieces.

Don't make a scene. Don't say anything to upset the professor. Put the dog down and scram. Fast.

I could see Jack studying the cages, the microscope, the test tubes; his expression as confused as mine.

"Get ready to run!" I whispered from the corner of my mouth. If I'd been closer I'd have grabbed him by the elbow and yanked him through the door.

Not getting my message—Jack's jaw set in a stubborn line.

Uh! Uh! Trouble!

I watched him square his shoulders and take a step forward. "Excuse me, Professor," he said politely. "What's with the weird lab? I hope you're not doing live tests on animals? 'Cos if you are—I'm dead against it. In fact, I'll report you to the police."

What was wrong with Jack? Couldn't he see we were in a big heap of trouble here? Didn't he realize we could be the professor's next experiments?

For several long silent seconds the professor gazed at Jack with strange unfocused eyes.

Ooh no…he was going to turn from Dr. Jekyll into Mr. Hyde. Any minute now he would burst through his clothing, develop muscles the size of dumbbells and sprout long black hair all over his body.

Without a word, the professor slowly reached into a drawer and drew out a pair of long shiny pointed scissors.

My eyes almost popped from my head.

Jack tripped over his feet as he took a hurried step backwards.

"Hey, if you feel that way, Professor," I gabbled, my throat dry with fear, my heart racing like an out-of-control motorboat, "we don't know a thing."

The professor put the scissors on the table and took out a small steel bowl and a bottle of disinfectant.

"Seeing as you are here," he said, his voice quiet and dead flat. "You may as well make yourselves useful."

Like a snake his eyes held mine. "You," he said, "hold Pedro still while I clean and bandage his leg."

His hypnotic gaze fell on Jack. "And you…whoever you are… can finish feeding Alex." He indicated the bald baby bird squawking indignantly on the floor. "Remember though, after every mouthful of porridge, Alex needs his face wiped. You can use that damp cloth next to the bowl."

I couldn't believe it. There was something like amusement tugging at the corners of the professor's mouth now. Was he playing with us like a snake plays with a mouse before gobbling it up?

It seemed to take Jack a few moments to shake off the scissors-scare. At last he peered down at the gaping mouth of the hungry bird under his feet and shrugged his shoulders.

"Me? Yeah. Cool." Jack tried to dodge the baby cockatoo, fold his flapping arms and legs and lower himself to the floor—and almost sat in the bowl of porridge.

"Ever heard of a native animal sanctuary?" With a gentle hand the professor bathed the blood and dirt from Pedro's leg and applied some sort of yellow disinfectant to the wound.

Geez…what was this scary man hinting at? Finding a nearby animal sanctuary so he could feed us to the crocodiles?

"Um—I guess it's a place that looks after native animals, like koalas, kangaroos and bilbies."

"Right. But *my* sanctuary will have native birds and reptiles too," added the professor as he deftly wrapped a white gauze bandage around Pedro's back leg.

And then the professor smiled at me. A smile that lit his

face up—like a Christmas tree, when you turned on the colored lights.

"Contrary to what you think—I am *not* a mad professor."

Could have fooled me.

"I am setting up a small sanctuary for all native fauna," he went on, his glance resting on the animals in their cages. "I have the council's approval, the funding is in place and in a few weeks' time the builders will arrive. They will build runs and shelters for these little creatures to live in when they are old enough."

"And the laboratory?"

Ugggh…Jack couldn't let it go, could he?

"Simple. I am a Professor of Veterinary Science. No good running an animal sanctuary without veterinary back-up."

"But why eggs?" Jack asked. "Why not full-grown animals?"

"These little darlings were born here. They won't miss the wild because they have no knowledge of it. Isn't that better than capturing full-grown animals, birds and reptiles and subjecting them to the trauma of captivity?"

Okay, I could go along with that. But I was still confused.

"Animals don't hatch from eggs," I argued. "Only birds and reptiles."

"It is surprising the number of people who think that." Filling a syringe with something from a small bottle, the professor injected Pedro, then picked him up and settled him into an empty cage lined with shredded paper. "There are three Australian egg-laying mammals. The platypus, and two species of Echidna."

Excitement bubbled inside of me.

"Echidnas? Can we see a baby echidna?"

"None have hatched yet, I am afraid. However, there are six echidna eggs under heat lamps in the shed. Maybe there will be a new-born puggle for you to see next time you come."

"Puggle?"

"That is what baby echidnas are called," he said, "Even a baby platypus is sometimes called a puggle. Here, help me put these little guys back to bed."

Bending down he scooped one baby platypus up in his hand and passed it to me.

"Put him in the end cage, the one with the blanket over it. Platypuses prefer the dark."

I looked down at the creature sitting in the palm of my hand. So warm—so odd looking. Afraid I'd squash the tiny bundle, I carried it carefully to the end cage and placed it on the clean straw.

"Later I will add other native animals, like kangaroos, wallabies and koalas to the sanctuary. Baby animals that have lost their mother," the professor continued as he put the other two platypuses to bed. "But this lot will be enough to get me started."

"Wow!" said Jack, looking completely blown away. "All

those eggs in the shed. They'll hatch into snakes and lizards and other cool stuff. Right?"

"That is right. Now, I think Alex has had enough porridge." The professor picked up the baby cockatoo from the floor, wiped him down and settled him back in his cage. "You too, Larry," he said, unhooking the lizard from his coat and tucking him into another cage with three other baby blue-tongues. "And I think it's time I walked you two children back to the front gate. You don't want the riding school to send out a search party. Do you?"

While we walked, Jack bombarded the Professor with questions about the sanctuary. He didn't even stop talking when Barnaby trotted up behind him and butted his pocket, looking for more carrots.

You know, one thing I've always liked about Jack—when he gets caught up in a project, he always gives it his full attention.

12

One eye on the stable clock, I pulled a notebook from my horse gear bag and flicked it open at the page headed: 'Professor's Egg Mystery'. The cartoony horse's head on the front of my horse gear bag glared at me. 'Hurry-up-you'll-be-late-for-Kate's-lesson', the glare seemed to say. Turning my back on the bag, I read the following:

Why does the professor have so many 'No Trespassing' signs on his property?

What is he hiding?

Is he an egg smuggler?

Does he have a mean accomplice hidden somewhere nearby?

Why does the professor need a people-eating bull to keep trespassers away?

Do platypuses hatch looking like pink jellybeans?

Okay, most of these questions had been answered…sort of. But was I missing something? My gut feeling kept telling me the professor and his eggs weren't as squeaky clean as he made out. Yet, his explanation made sense. Starting a native sanctuary by hatching the eggs was an environmentally friendly way to go.

Still deep in thought, I returned the notebook to the bag, picked up my riding helmet and crammed it on my head. Truth was—I didn't really want to let go of the professor's egg mystery. Deep down I didn't want him to be a vet instead of a mad scientist.

How was I supposed to write another Rebecca Turnbull P.I. mystery when there was no mystery to solve?

Rebecca Turnbull tightened the belt on her pale peach trench coat. She slipped on a pair of soft leather gloves and strode out into the cold night-air, her fierce Doberman, Fang, panting at her heels.

She was bored.

Bored. Bored. Bored.

Her mobile phone wasn't ringing. The police hadn't contacted her for weeks. No convenient dead body had turned up on a park bench or in a cupboard or dropped from a tree.

Seriously, if she didn't land a new case soon, she'd resort to buying a king-size container of double-chocolate-mud ice cream and sharing the tub with Fang...

I had three minutes to get ready for Kate's group lesson. Taking extra care, I fastened Shakespeare's tendon boots and stood up. Yesterday, one boot fell off as I trotted over the trot poles. Instead of blaming me, Kate blamed Noah for not showing me how to fasten the boots correctly. But it wasn't Noah's fault—he was a stickler for safety.

Funny thing, the more I had to do with Noah, the more I was able to put up with him. Okay he'd never be best friend material and was still *Short Dark and Very Irritating*, but he did have his good points. He was a mega-good teacher. So it beats me how the tendon boot just up and jumped off Shakespeare's leg. Perhaps my mind had been on the professor's eggs instead of on pressing all the Velcro straps down firmly.

Oh well, that wouldn't happen again. My mind could now focus on the task of riding, because according to the professor, he was cleaner than a brand new pair of Billabong jeans. Although come to think of it…where had all his eggs come from in the first place? You can't buy platypus eggs from the post-office—cockatoo eggs from the chemist—or lizard eggs from the library.

I still thought the professor was way weird.

But now it was time to surprise Kate with my new riding skills. Show her how much I'd improved since she'd first thrown me on Shakespeare and I'd fallen straight off the other side.

According to the notice on the communal bulletin board, today's lesson was going to be all about 'jumping into water'. Should be fun.

"Okay, let's show everyone how to do it," I told Shakespeare, kissing him on the softest, pinkest spot on his nose. His reply was to rub his head on the front of my shirt and then grab one of the buttons with his teeth.

"Hey, stop that!" Laughing, I pushed him away. I'd never seen Shakespeare looking so happy. Since he'd been out of retirement he was a different horse. I thought of Grandpa Ryan in the retirement home at Tanunda and swallowed a lump. Nothing to do—and all day to do it in. Lately, every time we visited him, Grandpa seemed older and more far-away.

With my helmet fastened under my chin, I led Shakespeare out of the stable block. First I tightened the girth one more hole, then, satisfied everything was secure, put my foot in the stirrup and swung up onto his back.

"Hi, Tayla."

As my best friend rode toward me, I blinked. Her whiter than white, crisp cotton shirt and dazzlingly shiny riding boots had me squinting in the sun. Geez…a mere mortal like me definitely needed sunglasses around this girl.

When Tayla halted beside me I could see she wasn't a happy little vegemite. Her face was the color of wet cement.

"You okay?"

"I'm going to be sick," she moaned. "I am sooo scared."

"Why?"

"What if I fall off in the water?"

"Come on, Tay, it's no big deal. If you fall off, just shake the water out of your eyes and get back on again." I grinned. "It'll be cool."

The color of her face didn't change—evidently she didn't get my pun. "I love riding Angel," she said, her voice small, "but jumping's way too scary."

For someone who was terrified of spiders, bugs and seeing dead people, this didn't surprise me.

It was weird, but I was actually looking forward to Cross-Country day. As well as riding bareback to strengthen my seat, Noah had shown me how to stand with a soccer ball between my legs. The trick was to keep squeezing the ball until you couldn't squeeze any more. His theory was that the exercise strengthened the calves and thighs. Whatever. As long as it stopped me from falling off so much.

By the time Tayla and I rode across to the working arena, the other ten riders had straggled into a wavy line. Like a sergeant major Kate stood in front, legs apart, hands behind her back, fair hair covered by a battered old Akubra hat.

"Okay, class," she said, lifting a 'you're late!' eyebrow at Tayla and me. "Line up in your groups."

We'd been divided into three teams on the first day of our holidays. Jack, Tayla, Sarah and I were the *Superheroes*. The other two teams were the *Sparticans* and the *Poppets*. One led by Tim Mathers, a real cute fourteen-year old who looked like Leonardo de Caprio's kid brother, and the other by Mandy Standish, a long-legged smiley girl who encouraged her team-mates like a cheer-leader, by yelling, *'Hop! Hop! Poppets are on top!'*.

Kate waited until we lined up behind our group leaders before continuing.

"Today you're going to jump the water-jump,' she told us. "But to get the horses warmed up, we'll play a game first. I want every member of each team, one at a time, to canter slowly toward the other end of the paddock. When you hear me fire my starter gun, spin on the spot and gallop back here as fast as you can. First back gets ten points for his or her team. Right? Leaders first, then we'll go down the line until everyone's had a turn. The game's called, 'Bang and go Back!' Any questions?"

"What if your horse breaks into a trot on the way out?" asked Mandy.

"You're disqualified."

"Why?"

Sarah, eyes rolling, butted in. "Because trotting is slower than cantering. If you're trotting when the gun goes bang you'd be closer to the finish when we spin and that would be cheating."

After an hilarious half hour spent yelling encouragement to our team members, cantering so slowly most of us got disqualified for breaking back into a trot, then spinning when the starter gun went bang and pretending we were jockeys galloping to the finishing line, we stopped for a break.

"Right," said Kate after a ten minute rest. "Back on your horses everyone and walk quietly over to the Cross-Country course. I'll meet you in front of jump number eight."

The time had come to either *jump* or *sit in* the water-jump.

Kate instructed us to jump obstacles six and seven first before tackling number eight. "Don't worry about the water jump," she said. "It's easy. Just use lots of leg, keep your pony straight, then pop over the log and trot out through the water on the other side. Simple as eating a Mars bar."

Of course our team had to go first. I could see Sarah looking edgy. Probably couldn't wait to show us what a star she was. Tayla's eyes were glazed over like she was pretending she was at home reading a self-help book instead of sitting on a horse. Jack's freckles stood out like beacons on a light-house. Me...I'd worked out a sure-fire plan. *Close my eyes and leave everything to Shakespeare.* I figured at twenty four, he'd been around a lot longer than me, so if he didn't know how to jump the log and splash through the water, I may as well go change into flippers now.

Naturally, Sarah made it look easy. She jumped six and seven as though they were poles on the ground, cantered up to the log, popped over into the water and trotted out again.

Grrrrrrrrr!

Fair dinkum, if Sarah didn't lose that smug smirk in the next minute and a half, I'd be forced to secretly scrub the toilet bowl with her toothbrush.

I could see Tayla's hands shaking on the reins as she walked Angel out of the line. Her eyes were huge. Her face had lost its wet-cement grey color but was now almost as white as her shirt.

"You can do it, Tayla," I whispered. "Just hang on and let Angel do the work."

Her jumping was shaky. It was scrambly. It was mega-slow. But at the end of three agonizing minutes, Tayla trotted back to the line, her smile wider than the Sydney Harbour Bridge. She'd made it around safely.

Jack's plan must have been 'the faster you gallop the sooner you finish'. I held my breath and watched him hurtle over the first two jumps then gallop toward the water jump as though chased by a sheriff's posse. And then, at the last moment, his plan backfired. Ferret, his horse, screeched to a halt and dug its hooves into the ground, as though to say, 'no way', while Jack kept going— over the log and into the water. It was like a tidal wave hitting the shore.

Ka-splash

Okay…I'd learned from watching Tayla and Jack. Not too slow and not too fast. Somewhere in between. Teeth clenched, heart bumping like a car on a rough road, I headed Shakespeare for jump six, a fence made from old car tires.

Shakespeare broke into a comfortable rocking-horse canter and the jump was so smooth I hardly felt the lift before we were on the other side and heading for the wooden bridge and the little jump made out of forty-four gallon drums.

Back to a brisk trot for the bridge. As we clip-clopped across, I imagined the big bad troll dripping water as he poked his head over the railing and growled, "Who's that tripping over my bridge?"

Of course I'd tell him it was only the *Little* Billy-goat Gruff and if he hung around for a little longer, there'd be lots more big fat tasty goats following me.

Once on the other side, Shakespeare cleared the drums with a kick and an arrogant flick of his tail.

Hey, this was fun...

Back into that lovely rocking-horse canter, I gathered up my reins and aimed him at the water jump.

Time to close my eyes and leave it to the horse.

It was like sitting on an active volcano. Shakespeare bunched himself beneath me and exploded into the air. *Kaapow!* Was it a bird or a plane or a Super-Cha? Okay, I lost both stirrups, clung on like a burr with my soccer-ball strengthened legs and wrapped both arms around Shakespeare's outstretched neck to keep from falling off— but hey, what a feeling!

Opening one eye, I glanced down at the water far below. Not content with popping over the log into the water, Shakespeare jumped the log *and* the water in one bound. He landed like a cat, a good two meters on the other side, and slowed to an ambling trot, then to a shuffling walk and with a smug, Sarah-like-smirk, strolled back to his gob-smacked fans.

Kate was the first to recover.

"Oh you beautiful boy! You clever beautiful boy!"

While I slid my feet back into the stirrups, Kate threw her arms around Shakespeare's neck. I could see tears trickling down her cheeks.

"You haven't forgotten, have you?" Kate's voice sounded scratchy. "Just like when you took me over that horrific water jump at the World Cup Show jumping finals in Switzerland."

And then it hit me…

All those pictures lining the walls in Kate's office of a beautiful dark grey horse called, 'The Tempest' leaping over huge fences with a young and pretty Kate aboard…

That was Shakespeare.

Grumpy, bony old Shakespeare was 'The Tempest'.

13

That night I had a bad dream.

Or should I say a horrible freaky nightmare. You know, where everything that's happening seems so real. Where your heart slams and crashes around like a trapped animal and threatens to burst through your chest. Where you try to call out for your mum but the only thing that comes out of your mouth is a skinny grey rat that gives you the evil eye then scuttles away to its hole.

Anyway…this dream started where I was cantering along on Shakespeare and we were both smelling the flowers and enjoying the sunshine. Everything was perfect—until we came across Professor Goodenough's egg shed. For no reason at all, Shakespeare snorted in fright then took off in one of his huge sky-scraper leaps.

At the height of the jump, I looked down. It was totally weird. I could see through the roof of the shed to where all the professor's eggs had suddenly sprouted wings. And there was Pedro, yapping like a squeaky wheel and having a great time running around on his cotton-reel legs playing chasy with the flying eggs.

Suddenly, from who-knows-where, this gigantic egg appeared. It split open with a bang and out stepped a baby dinosaur. Thick leathery wings. Fire hiccupping from its mouth. Smell like a rubbish bin. Then—in the time it took for Pedro to blink in surprise—the creature ballooned to the size of an elephant.

"Don't touch Pedro, you great bully!" I screamed.

But it was too late. Like a giant vacuum cleaner, the dinosaur sucked the little dog down its throat.

My pulse racing and bucking in fear, I watched the monster lick his bloated lips and ever so slowly turn bloodshot eyes and dribbling grin toward me.

"Go Shakespeare!" I yelled flapping my legs on his sides.

Once again—I was too late.

I could hear Pedro's frantic yapping as the dinosaur opened his mouth wide and sucked Shakespeare and me inside. The little dog wouldn't stop yapping. He was racing up and down, banging into the dinosaur's ribs and head-butting his liver…

And that's when I woke up.

Not on my bed, but thrashing around on the floor, sheets twisted around both legs, pillow damp with sweat.

After untangling the sheets, I decided the nightmare must mean Pedro was in danger. Perhaps the professor was using him in some weird experiment. Perhaps he'd replaced the dog's injured leg with a robotic one. Whatever…it was time to pay the professor another visit.

However, before I could check up on Pedro, I had my

lesson with Noah to get through.

Strangely, this morning's lesson went well. Noah kept giving me the thumbs up sign. Even yelled 'Great!' and 'Good!' a couple of times which almost made me fall off my horse in surprise. I guess his good mood had something to do with Kate lifting the ban on his riding after I'd managed to stay on Shakespeare over the water jump.

As soon as the lesson finished I went hunting for Jack. No way was I going anywhere near the egg-shed by myself. I needed my No.1 assistant to help scare away the nightmare.

But Jack had gone for a ride to Gawler River with his new mate, Tim Mathers.

Okay, my No. 2 assistant would have to come with me.

I found Tayla in our room putting the finishing touches to a hat she was making for Angel. She'd cut two holes in an old straw hat for the pony's ears, added ribbon and plastic daisies to the crown, then glued purple sprinkles around the brim.

I dug up my sweetest smile and sat on the bed beside her. "That's way cool," I gushed. "Angel will love it."

"You don't think it's too over the top for her do you?"

"Nah. The purple sprinkle stuff will definitely bring out the color of her eyes." I widened my smile and cracked my fingers—then changed the subject. "You know how little Pedro hurt his leg?"

Tayla's look was wary. "Pedro? The professor's dog?"

"Yeah. Poor little guy."

"What about him?"

"I think he might be in trouble."

"And?"

"I need to go see if he's okay." I grabbed her hand. "Please, Tay, come with me."

Tayla pulled away and jumped off the bed so quickly, I had to hold onto the headboard to stop from bouncing onto the floor.

"No way! I'm not going anywhere near that crazy old man. And don't try talking me into it, Chiana. Nothing you say will change my mind."

"We'll only stay for five minutes. Come on Tayla. It's important. I really need to check on little Pedro."

Tayla backed away as though I'd suddenly come down with rabies. "Watch my lips, Cha. N. O. You'd have to tie me up and drag me all the way to get me to come with you."

She must have sensed I was considering her suggestion because she dropped onto the bed as though her legs wouldn't hold her up any more.

"Come on, Tayla," I persisted before deciding to change tactics. After all, I *was* desperate. "You owe me one."

"Owe you? What for?"

"If my mum and Ken hadn't gone on their honeymoon, where would you be right now?'

"Huh?" Tayla's eyes seemed to glaze over in confusion.

"You'd be at home. Bored out of your brain. That's

where you'd be. Probably listening to your latest CD for the seven hundredth time."

Tayla twisted Angel's straw hat until one of the daisies fell off onto the floor.

"Instead of that,' I continued, giving her my best hurt-friend look. "You've spent these holidays riding the sweetest pony at *Treehaven*."

Ahaa…hit a nerve there.

"I'm right, aren't I?" I continued relentlessly. "Admit it. So the least you can do in return is come with me while I take some black jellybeans to poor little Pedro and make sure he's okay. Five minutes of your time. That's not too much to ask of a friend, is it?"

"But—"

"And as for being afraid of the professor—why, he's just a sweet old man who's setting up a sanctuary for orphaned animals."

"Er…well…"

Mission accomplished.

However, ten minutes later, when Tayla sighted the rolls of razor wire and realized I expected her to wriggle underneath, I had an even bigger battle on my hands.

"Me? Wriggle under there? You've got to be kidding," she said eyeballing me in disbelief. "Isn't there a bell or a buzzer or something we can ring?"

"Look, it's easy," I said throwing myself flat on the ground. "Just pretend you're a snake."

"I'm scared of snakes!"

"Okay, a river flowing under a bridge."

Honestly, Tayla could be *such* hard work.

By the time we'd 'flowed' under the fence Barnaby had wandered over to nose in my pocket for carrots.

"Meet my new friend, Barnaby," I said, introducing the bull to a bug-eyed Tayla. "And Barnaby, this is my best friend in the whole world, Tayla."

Barnaby smiled and drooled and munched his way through the carrot he'd found in my pocket. That is, after spitting out my mobile which he'd grabbed by mistake.

Tayla choked. "Holy catfish! Who sharpened the points on that bull's horns?"

"Barnaby's okay," I said. "As long as you feed him carrots and never *ever* run."

As we came closer, I could see the Professor's sprawling old house with the veranda running along the front. Scarred wooden posts, overflowing with dark green ferns, stood each side of the veranda steps.

"Is that the professor?" whispered Tayla grabbing my arm. "That old man with the gross beard arguing with a young guy near the shed?"

"Yes, that's him," I whispered back. Don't know why we bothered whispering because both men were arguing so loudly they wouldn't have heard us if we'd driven up in a tractor.

"We have to get that egg. Today. Before it is too late," the professor shouted.

"That's impossible. It's too dangerous, Gramps."

Gramps?

I tugged Tayla behind some bushes for cover. There was something familiar about the man in faded jeans and leather jacket. I'd seen him somewhere before. But where?

"Tayla," I said. "Does that young guy look familiar to you?"

She didn't answer. Just stared at me, eyes dark and fearful, breath coming in short quick gulps. And then she nodded.

"Well...who is it?"

When she spoke, her voice sounded croaky, hard to get out. "I-It's the greasy-haired guy who bumped into you at the museum—just before the dinosaur egg disappeared."

This time it was my turn to stare and gulp.

Oh...My...God! Of course!

And the greasy-haired guy had just called the professor Gramps!

14

Professor Goodenough had lied to us.

Not only had he stolen the native eggs in the shed but he must have master-minded the theft of the fossilized baby *Therizinosaur* as well. I'd been taken in by his gooey, smiley, honey-sweet face when he'd watched the baby platypus hatching. Huh! And all the time he'd been silently counting the dollars the new baby would add to his bank account after he'd smuggled it out of the country.

I crept closer so I could hear the professor and Greasy-Hair's plans. By the look on Tayla's face, she'd rather be taking off in the other direction. I guess the only thing that stopped her was the thought of Barnaby and no carrots.

She grabbed my jacket and pulled. "Cha, we've got to go tell Kate. Get her to ring the police."

"And what will we tell them? That we saw Greasy-Hair at the museum the day the egg disappeared? Hey, we saw hundreds of people at the museum that day. We have to get more evidence. More proof. We have to find out where they've hidden the dinosaur egg."

"I knew it!" Tayla hid her face in her hands. I watched her rock herself back and forward then sit on the ground and curl her arms around her chest. "I knew this would happen if I came with you. I just knew it!"

The professor locked the shed door and turned to his grandson.

"We'll bring the egg back here and hide it in amongst the other eggs. It will be safe with me."

"But will *you* be safe, Gramps?"

Professor Goodenough put his hand in his pocket and, like a magician producing a white rabbit, pulled out Pedro.

"Barnaby and Pedro will look after me. No-one sets foot on this property without them letting me know. And by that time I will have my trusty shotgun loaded and ready to fire."

Pedro, his back leg still bandaged, blinked his eyes sleepily, yawned and looked around. Suddenly his little black eyes lit up and his tail went into spasms of joy. Oh no! *Please, Pedro, don't come over here and give us away.*

"Pedro!" barked the professor. "Sit! Guard the shed. Stay!"

The little dog's ears and tail drooped and he gave me one last mournful glance before slinking back and sitting down in front of the shed door.

"Whether you help me or not, I'm getting the *Therizinosaur* egg." The professor opened the car door and eased himself onto the seat. "Well—are you coming with me—or am I going on my own?"

"Man, if you weren't so old and skinny, I'd string you up and use you for target practice, you cantankerous old buzzard." Greasy-Hair, fists clenched, his face red, stormed over to the passenger side of the car, opened the door and slammed it so hard behind him the hinges jiggled up and down. "If you go putting your nose where it's not wanted—I'm warning you—you'll be a dead man."

"He's talking bodies. I'm going to be sick." Tayla buried herself further into the middle of the bush as the ute rumbled and farted into life.

"Here's my last carrot," I whispered, eyes on the crooks' vehicle. "Use it to get past Barnaby then go back and tell the others. Tell Jack to have his mobile switched on. If I get into trouble I'll ring."

"What? Cha! No!"

I waited until the ute chugged past then ducked out from behind the bush and swung up onto the back, praying neither Greasy-Hair nor the Professor could see me in the rear-view mirror. I was in luck—they were too busy quarrelling.

Two bales of straw lay in the back of the ute so I curled up between them and pulled a scratchy hessian bag over my body. The last I saw of Tayla was her chalky face and her wide open mouth.

Hey! If the professor and his grumpy grandson were off to pick up the stolen dinosaur egg, so was I. If I could catch them 'at it'—that's all the proof I'd need.

<h1 style="text-align:center">15</h1>

About ten minutes later, I felt the ute come to a clanking halt. I had truck size bruises on one arm—an egg-shaped lump on my head from a loose hammer that crashed from one side to the other each time the car lumbered around a corner—and I smelt of old birds. No wonder. The sack I'd hidden under was covered in dried feathers and chicken poo.

Where were we?

Cautiously I poked my head out from under the smelly sack. The professor had parked over the road from a large galvanized iron warehouse with 'Simpson's Importers & Exporters' printed in bold black lettering across the front of the building. Underneath was their slogan, printed in red: 'At Simpson's we export/import—anything—anywhere'.

Did that mean they were smugglers?

Before I could escape from the back of the ute, Greasy-Hair started yelling at his grandfather. "You stay here, Gramps, and don't move. Got it? Otherwise," he went on, climbing out of the car and slamming the door behind him, "you'll end up as crocodile bait. Fingers and Meathead almost caught you last time you tried to get in."

"But—" began the professor.

"You cantankerous old fool…" Greasy-Hair banged his fist down on the roof of the cabin and spat from the side of his mouth. "Didn't you hear me? If you're caught snooping around inside the warehouse you'll get us *both* killed. I'll nick the egg for you—but only if you do as I say. Wait for fifteen minutes and if I'm not back by then—get the hell outta here. Right?"

The stomp of his boots bit into the bitumen as he crossed the road toward the warehouse. Once again I lifted my head from under the sack and wriggled across the hard metal floor to the edge of the tray. The moment Greasy-Hair disappeared inside the building, I swung off the edge and hunched down behind the car.

A minute later I poked my head around the back tire and eyed the driver's side door. What would the professor do? Would he 'stay put' or risk becoming 'crocodile bait'?

And what about me?

Could I follow Greasy-Hair without the professor noticing me?

Music, slow and wailing, drifted from the window of the car. Good. The professor was staying put.

Now was a good time to let my assistants know my whereabouts. That's more P.I. talk. While the professor's slow, sad music covered any noise I might make, I pulled out my mobile and pressed Jack's number. Immediately a voice answered—

"Noah?" I squeaked. "What are *you* doing with Jack's mobile?"

"Mum's got Jack helping her with the computer. He gave me his phone and told me to stand by for your call. What's going on? Where are you?"

"I'm at Simpson's warehouse."

"I know Simpson's. It's this side of Gawler," said Noah. "Now, what's happening? Are you in any trouble?"

"Only if I get caught. There's a couple of mean-sounding guys called Fingers and Meathead inside the warehouse. I could be in trouble if *they* see me."

"How will they see you if you're outside Simpsons?" growled Noah.

"'Cos I'm going in."

"No, Cha. Wait till *we* get there. The horses are saddled and waiting and as soon as we rescue Jack—we're on our way." Noah sounded as though he was enjoying this cloak and dagger stuff. Hey, he might make a good P.I. assistant after all. And then he spoiled the image by opening his mouth one more time. "So…don't do anything stupid before we get there!"

The phone went dead. I couldn't believe it. *Short Dark and Irritating* had hung up on me.

From behind the ute I peered across at Simpson's warehouse. A truck and four powerful-looking motorbikes were parked on the road outside. I could see a delivery man loading boxes into the back of the truck.

When he finished he waved to a guy dressed in khaki overalls who'd been helping him, then he drove off. Seemed like any other warehouse to look at, but what was happening inside? Was Simpson using his business as a smuggling cover-up? Or were Greasy-Hair and his mates using the export-import company as a cover, stealing native eggs and smuggling them overseas without the owner knowing?

Should I go in? Or should I wait for back-up? If I waited—it might be too late. Greasy-Hair said he'd be out in fifteen minutes.

I tugged at a loose piece of nail with my teeth. What would Rebecca Turnbull do if she were in my shoes?

Rebecca Turnbull came to a screeching halt outside the warehouse. She had two loaded guns in the pocket of her apricot trench coat and a knife tucked in the top of her brown suede boot. Putting on her tinted sunnies with diamonds set in each corner, she swung herself over the car door. With a mighty leap, her trained-to-kill Doberman, Fang, leaped to the footpath and stood beside her. Teeth set in a snarl, the dog led the way into the warehouse.

Φ

Fingers was the first to go down. Fang had him pinned to the ground within seconds; his jagged teeth playing a tune on the thug's throat. When Meathead took a swing at Rebecca, she caught his fist like it was a soccer ball and bounced him against the wall. Greasy-Hair ran screaming back to his Grandpa...

Φ

Yep! That's what Rebecca Turnbull would do.

I let out a sigh.

But not Chiana Ryan...

Getting inside the warehouse was easy enough. No scary guy grabbed me. No-one said, 'Get lost, kid, or I'll use your head for a dart-board.' In fact, everyone was too busy working to notice me. Men and women dressed in khaki overalls scurried around like ants at a picnic, packing shredded paper into boxes, banging nails into wooden boxes, pasting addresses on the side of boxes or lifting and carrying boxes on bright yellow fork-lifts.

I spotted Greasy-Hair turning into a passageway off the main warehouse and followed him, P.I. style. That is, I pulled the collar up on my jacket, tugged my imaginary hat down over my eyes and darted quick looks first over one shoulder then the other, before scurrying after him.

Half way along the passageway, he shoved open a door with *Gymnasium* written in big black letters across the front. I blinked. *Gymnasium*? Surely I hadn't risked my life riding in the back of that rusty ute, only to end up spying on a guy while he lifted weights and did push-ups?

"Yo, Fingers! What ya know, man?" My target's voice, greasy as his hair, floated through the inch of space between the door and the doorway.

I pressed one eyeball to the opening. The room was fitted out like a real gym. Bench presses, weights, bikes, treadmills—the lot. Two men the size of hippos were lifting weights near the door. Their sweat smelt like rotten potatoes. Their grunts sounded like they were having trouble going to the toilet.

I could tell which one was Fingers—one hand had none—fingers that is. The other guy had a head the size and color of a side of lamb. Meathead I guess.

"Boss is lookin' for you, Arty," grunted Fingers lifting an iron bar that probably weighed as much as a horse.

"Boss says you've been a naughty boy," added the other guy.

I did a double take. Meathead's body, ogre-like and covered with tattoos and black hair could have belonged to an ape or a wrestler, but his voice sounded high and squeaky like a little kid.

Greasy-Hair, or should I say, Arty, fiddled with the lock on a door at the back of the room. He turned around, an evil grin on his face. "That makes three of us, doesn't it?"

"Boss not happy," continued Meathead's babyish voice. "Says he's found stuff out about you."

"Yeah?" growled Arty opening the door of the back room and slipping inside. "Probably heard about all the guys I killed back in Tasmania."

I'd traveled in the back of the ute with a killer?

Fingers grunted and dropped his weights on the floor. Luckily the floor was cement so the weights just groaned and bounced instead of disappearing through a great big hole in the wood.

He shambled across to the bench-press. "Watchadoin' in there, Arty? Ya know the boss don't like anyone in his office."

"I'm just checking on something he wants me to ship off tomorrow. Interesting export. There could be a bit of money in it for us."

I'd heard enough. These three were dastardly crooks—smugglers. And they were using an honest company as cover.

As I tried to close the door quietly, it slipped from my fingers. To my ears the resulting click sounded as loud as a gunshot. I held my breath. Squeezed my eyes shut. Had they heard the noise? Were Fingers and Meathead getting ready to crash through the door without opening it, drag me inside the gym and practice kick-boxing with my head? Was Greasy-Hair planning to pull off his first murder in South Australia?

I opened my eyes. Snatched a look up and down the passageway. No voices. No crashing doors. No murderous yells. Okay, should I tell the boss what I'd heard or get out of here pronto and go find a policeman?

As I tiptoed along the grey cement passageway I heard a woman's voice speaking from behind one of the closed doors.

"Yes, sir," the lilting voice said. "Arthur Goodenough is in the gym. I saw him go past. Would you like him paged?"

"No, Marcia. Leave him to me. Just inform all employees

the gym is closed for the remainder of the day. No-one—I repeat *no-one* is to use the gym today." The man's voice was smooth, authoritative. Must be the boss. When he came out, I'd let him know about the crooks.

I squared my shoulders and stood waiting for the owner of the authoritative voice to push through the doorway. Wouldn't he be surprised to learn Greasy-Hair and his two muscle bound mates were smugglers? Probably give me a reward.

Suddenly, without warning, someone—or something—slammed into me from behind. The wind thumped from my chest. I lost my footing and stumbled forward. But before I could scream, a large rough hand clamped over my mouth. Strong, digging-in fingers grabbed me by the arm and dragged me toward the nearest doorway. I kicked out, my toes crunching against the wooden door as it closed behind us. Ignoring the pain, I kept kicking backwards until the toe of one riding boot came up hard against my attacker's shin.

Bullseye!

The strong smell of garlic and a low *Ooof* came from behind me. Was I in the clutches of a kidnapper? A murderer? Heart racing and gasping for air, I inched my head backwards until I found myself staring into the furious eyes of Greasy-Hair…Arty Goodenough. His scowl could have turned milk sour and he looked like he was itching to turn me into fish bait.

16

"**W**ho the hell are you, kid?" Greasy-Hair growled. "And what were you doing listening outside the gym door?"

The room we were in was not much bigger than a closet and smelt of disinfectant, musty mops and dust. Probably a cleaner's store-room. If only I could wriggle out from under his bulldog grip, I could yell for help. Failing that, I might be able to reach forward with my leg and kick the door to attract someone's attention.

I squirmed and kicked out, but his hand, digging into my cheekbones, pressed down even harder. Swearing under his breath he pulled me further into the room until his back was pressed up against the wall.

"Shhh!" he hissed. "Not a sound or we'll *both* be dead meat."

Like I believed that.

"Were you following me, kid? Or did Fingers put you up to this?" he asked, each whispered word a tickle of spit in my ear.

I grunted and rolled my eyes. Under his hand, my breathing was growing ragged and my nose and eyes were watering. If he wanted answers, we'd either have to talk in eye-rolls or he'd have to give me some breathing space. I tried to snag a deep breath and couldn't. What if my nose blocked up altogether and I couldn't breathe at all?

He must have seen the panic in my eyes because his hand loosened a little. "Look, kid. I'm the good guy. I'm a policeman working under-cover to investigate an egg smuggling ring."

Yeah. Right. And I'm a fairy princess!

Once again he must have read my thoughts because he snatched his police badge and card from inside the top of his boot and shoved it under my nose.

"Now, if I take my hand away from your mouth will you promise not to make a sound? They're bad guys out there and wouldn't think twice about doing away with a nosy kid as well as a cop."

I nodded. Cop or killer—I needed air.

The rough authoritative voice I'd heard before drifted under the door. "I'll be in the gym for quite a while, Marcia. No phone calls. No disturbances. And if you hear any screams or strange noises—ignore them. Understand?"

"Of course, Mr. Simpson."

"That's the boss." Arty screwed up his face—made him look like he'd bitten into a wormy apple and swallowed the worm. "If he finds us—we're toast."

Seconds after the footsteps passed our door, Arty dug his hand into an inside pocket of his coat then turned to me. I felt a lump rising in my throat, tasted fear in my mouth as my eyes fixed on the black handled revolver in his hand.

"It's okay, kid. Don't be scared," he soothed, squeezing my shoulder. "This is just insurance—in case I have no other way of getting you out safely."

He inched the door open a crack, snuck a quick look outside, then closed it again. "Can't escape that way. Marcia's standing outside her office flirting with the foreman." He turned to me, eyebrows dragging downwards. "You didn't tell me who you are and how the hell you got here."

"I'm Chiana—I'm a sort of friend of your grandfather. I caught a ride here in the back of his ute."

He looked confused. "Why?"

"Why?" I repeated slowly. Good question. With killers on the outside of the door and a guy with a gun standing beside me, I couldn't work out why either. "I—well…I thought you and your grandfather were egg thieves."

"Egg thieves?"

"Remember—you bumped into me at the museum just before the dinosaur egg went missing. And what about the professor? He has all those weird eggs in his shed, so I thought—"

"Grandpa and his obsession with that dinosaur egg," Arty broke in. "It belongs to him, you know. His father, my great-grandfather, Cyril Goodenough, discovered the fossil while digging in the Adelaide hills and donated it to the State museum. Of course, when Grandpa heard the egg had been stolen, he went ballistic. And when he found out Eric Simpson, the boss of this company, intended smuggling his precious *Therizinosaur* to a client in Japan, he insisted I get the egg back." Arty ran his hand through his hair. "Now—between you and him—you've messed up the entire police operation."

"Sorry. I didn't know—"

A noise that sounded like a door being ripped off its hinges or two rhinos wrestling sounded outside the door. "Search every room! Tear everything apart! That traitor, Goodenough, can't have gone far."

"Yeah, boss. No worries. I told Arty you wouldn't like him bein' in your office. Didn't know he was nicking the egg though."

"Shut up, you moron, and go get him. Sugar says she saw him talking to some big knob detective yesterday and they were acting real friendly like. He's either a cop or a grass. I'll get Gonzo to make a nice pair of cement boots in Arty's size then we'll drop him in the river and see how far he can swim."

Arty, his face a mask, moved over to the cleaner's cupboard and pulled open the door.

"Get in here, kid," he whispered. "And stay there until this is over. They don't know you're here."

"But what about you?"

I could hear heavy footsteps getting closer. Another door slamming. Muffled grunts and more loud swearing.

"Don't worry about me, kid. Just do exactly as I say." He thrust a small parcel into my hand. "This is the dinosaur egg. Give it to Grandpa then ring the police. Ask for Detective Inspector John Gilman. Got it? John Gilman. He knows all about the operation. Tell him where I am and what's happened."

"But—"

"God, you're as stubborn as that cantankerous old man out in the car. Stay hidden in the cupboard. Then, when they take me away, get yourself out of the warehouse and follow my orders. Can you do that for me, Chiana?"

I put on my ready-for-anything P.I. face and stepped inside the cupboard. "You got it," I assured him as he closed the door behind me.

Two seconds later I heard an ear-splitting crash, a loud *Oof,* lots of yelling, then something or someone being dragged from the room.

17

Fifty one. Fifty two. Fifty three.

Counting in my head stopped me from breathing too loudly. Or screaming. Hand covering my mouth, I stared at the deep scratch marks on the inside of the scarred cupboard door, traced the shape of what looked like a skull and cross-bones with the tip of one finger.

Fifty four. Fifty five. Fifty six.

The smell of disinfectant was making me gag. Any minute now I'd chuck up all over the cleaner's mops and polishing rags.

Fifty seven. Fifty eight. Fifty nine.

A cold shiver sent goose-bumps galumphing down my arms. Noah was right. I should have waited for back-up. I was twelve years old—scared—close to vomiting. Who did I think I was? Rebecca Turnbull—twenty five, tough, and street-smart? Oh yeah—and a complete fragment of my imagination.

Once again, my heart did a leap-frog inside my chest. What if Meathead and Fingers were waiting on the other side of the cupboard door? What if they were waiting to bat a home run with my head when I poked it out?

Sixty.

Hardly daring to breathe, I inched open the cupboard door a chink and scanned the room with one wary eye.

Empty—except for the faint smell of garlic and what looked like splatters of blood on the grey tiled floor.

Arty's blood?

I didn't want to think about it. All I wanted to do was run.

After a quick glance along the passageway, I forced my legs to move slowly, one step at a time, into the main warehouse. The front door seemed a trillion miles away. I wanted to bolt toward it but knew I had to play it cool, not draw attention to myself. At every sudden sound or movement I jumped like a scared rabbit but no-one even glanced up as I walked by. The workers were as busy as ants stocking up for a long cold winter.

Six more steps and I'd be safe. Five…four…

"Hey, kid!"

I almost leapt through the roof. Two strides from the doorway a guy with a foreman-tag on the front of his grey coat put his hand on my shoulder. Was this Gonzo? Was this the guy who measured shoe sizes? Made cement boots for a living?

"You've no mind to be in her," Gonzo/foreman said through his stained yellow teeth. "Didn't you read the sign on the door? This is for workers only. If you want to place an order for your Dad or pick up brochures for a school project go around to the front office."

"O-oh, s-sorry, mister," I stuttered, shaking in relief.

Geez. This P.I. business was way too scary. There was a cop in the gymnasium being fitted with cement boots. I had a mega-million-year-old dinosaur egg in my pocket that the bad-guys would kill me for. And I'd gone and left my mobile phone in the cleaning-cupboard. I remember taking it out of my pocket, switching it to vibrate and then burying it under some towels in case the sudden noise gave away my hiding place.

Still shaking, I staggered outside, grabbed a gulp of fresh air and looked anxiously up and down the street. Where was the professor? Of course, Arty had told his grandpa to leave if he wasn't back in fifteen minutes. Although it felt like I'd been inside the warehouse for a year, my watch showed it was only half an hour.

With a nervous glance over my shoulder I pulled the collar of my jacket up and hurried along the street. No professor meant there was no car to make a getaway. No mobile phone meant I couldn't ring the police as Arty had ordered.

Things were looking black.

As I slipped around the corner of the warehouse, I could hear this totally awful singing. The song was about a dog called Shep and the singer had to shoot the dog because it was getting old. Totally sad and weird. But the good part—the music was coming from the professor's car. Yay! Never before had I been so pleased to see

Professor Goodenough or his beat up old ute. Against his grandson's orders, he'd stayed close by, just driven around the corner to wait.

I opened the passenger side door and dropped into the seat beside him.

"Let's scram," I said slamming the car door and fastening my seat belt.

The professor turned a blank face toward me.

"I'm Chiana from the riding school. Remember?"

He leaned over and switched off his tape-deck then turned to me with a slight frown. "Of course I remember you, Chiana. But I am sorry, I can't give you a lift, I am waiting for my grandson."

"Do you know where the nearest phone box is, Professor? I left my mobile inside the warehouse and we need to ring the police."

"Police?"

"Please. We have to get out of here. Arty's in big trouble—"

"*My* Arty?"

"Yes. Gonzo, the cement-boots man, could be after me too. Come on, professor, let's go!"

The professor, although shaking his head like it was full of cobwebs, turned the key in the ignition.

"The phone box is half a mile away," he said, doing up his seat-belt. "What's happened to my Arty? Is he hurt?"

"I don't know," I choked, trying to speak around the lump in my throat. "Your Arty saved my life. Made me hide in a cupboard so Fingers and Meathead wouldn't find me. Then there was a fight and I heard Arty being dragged away to the gym."

I couldn't tell the professor about the blood. I didn't even want to think about the blood.

One hand on the horn to warn a little green hatchback to move itself—*now*—the professor crunched the gears into top and roared fire-engine fast down the street.

"Arty gave me the *Therizinosaur*, Professor," I said, fingering the foam-packed box in my pocket. "He said to give it to you."

"What use is the egg to me if Arty gets hurt?" he asked. And then, more to himself, "I shouldn't have pestered him about the egg. It's my fault Arty's in trouble."

"It's not your fault, Professor. The boss found out Arty was a cop. Nicking the egg just made him a bit madder."

Neither of us spoke until we'd screeched to a halt in front of the public phone-box. While the professor emptied his pockets onto the hood of the car looking for coins, I pushed through the glass door and checked to see if the phone was in working order.

"No coins," bleated the professor, sounding like a lost sheep.

Turning out my pockets I found a fifty cent coin, two twenty cent coins and a half-eaten Mars bar.

"Here, Professor," I said handing over the money. "Arty said to ask for Detective Inspector John Gilman. That must be his boss."

While the professor made the call, I jigged up and down on the footpath; all the time watching out for Fingers and Meathead. If the deadly duo did come looking for me where could I hide? Under the car? Up a tree? Inside a rubbish bin?

Suddenly, over the hill, with the weak sunlight shining behind them, four horse riders appeared. Jack, Noah, Sarah and Tayla. Laughter bubbled in my throat as they waved and trotted toward me. My assistants had never looked so beautiful. Even Sarah, who had this sour—*you're-going-to-cop-it-when-I-tell-Mum*—expression on her face.

"Hey!" yelled Jack, his grin matching mine.

"Hey!" I yelled back.

"You okay?" growled Noah.

"No. They've got Arty. And now I think they're after me."

"Who's Arty? Who's *they*?" It was Tayla, confused, sort of sick looking, but definitely still part of the team.

"Arty's the professor's grandson. You know, Tayla, the Greasy-Hair guy from the museum. He's been working undercover for the police, but the crooks found out and they're fitting him for cement boots."

Noah stared down at me. "And now they're looking for you? But why?"

"I have the dinosaur egg."

"You've got what?" Jack's eyes shone. "Where?"

"In my—" I frowned. I'd suddenly caught sight of four motorbikes in the distance. Something about the way the riders hunched over their bikes, determined and down-to-business, made me freeze. There'd been four motorbikes outside the warehouse.

"Oh geez!" I gasped. "It's Fingers and Meathead and they've got back-up."

"Quick! Get on behind me!" Noah leaned over, grabbed my hand and yanked me up onto his horse.

I struggled to find my balance. "What about the professor? We can't leave him."

"No way am I getting on a horse," growled the professor as he let the door of the phone box swing shut behind him. "The police will be here any minute. Get going. I'll be alright."

"But—"

"Chiana! Go! These men don't know who I am. If you gallop across country, you might lose them." Using his stick to walk more quickly, he hurried to the car, wrenched open the door and slid inside. "Well, don't just stand there gaping. I said, go!"

The bikes roared closer.

"You heard the man!" yelled Tayla flicking Angel with her reins.

"And Chiana," said the professor, his voice a squeak. "Try not to break my egg."

These were the last words I heard before we galloped off. Mega fast. From whoa to go. And if I hadn't clutched Noah around the waist in a python-grip, I'd have slid right off his horse's back and landed on the bitumen.

<h1 style="text-align:center">18</h1>

The big chestnut show jumper leapt the stone wall and galloped on. With my arms wrapped around Noah's waist, I bounced up and down behind the saddle. I couldn't speak. I couldn't see where we were going. I could barely breathe.

Knowing the countryside around Gawler better than we did, Noah took the lead in our race against the motor bikes.

"Everyone still here?" he yelled over his shoulder.

Grunts and yells greeted his question. I could imagine Tayla shaking in her stirrups behind us. She loved riding Angel but was terrified of jumping—and yet here she was, galloping across country and jumping everything in her path. No wonder I was proud to have her for a best friend.

And what about Sarah? Somehow she'd been different since we arrived at *Treehaven*. Horses must agree with my contrary stepsister because she was friendlier now. Not such a pain in the butt.

And Jack—well, Jack was Jack. Always there. Always reliable. Always happy to be in the middle of a mystery.

"They're still following us," Sarah yelled as she galloped up beside Noah's chestnut. "They must have found an opening in the wall."

I glanced over my shoulder. The snarl of the bikes hit the air like wet towels on a windy day. Oil and smoke choked my nostrils. Screams and whines, like wild beasts intent on a kill, echoed around the countryside. In fact, the bikers were so close I could see their black helmets and leather jackets painted with strange red symbols on the front.

Yeah. We were in major trouble.

"Okay, here's the plan!" yelled Noah as the other riders caught up and galloped in a line beside us. "There's a dam up ahead. It's surrounded by trees so you can't see it until you're almost on top of it. What we're going to do is lead them into the water. Got it?"

"And what about us?" asked Jack.

"Remember the game we played in Kate's lesson? Bang and go back?"

"Yeah. So?"

"What we'll do is gallop in a line toward the water and the moment I yell *Bang,* spin around and gallop in the opposite direction. With any luck they won't see the water until it's too late."

The noise of the bikes ricocheted and boomed around us as shoulder to shoulder the horses hurtled toward the water. Unconsciously, I hung on tighter to Noah.

Closer. Closer.

"Bang!" Noah yelled at last, his voice scratchy.

Every horse spun as though in a ballet production. Sarah and Tayla galloped off to the right. Jack, Noah and I to the left.

And the bikes kept on going.

I grinned and whooped as the sound of four individual splashes were followed by loud yells and colorful swearing. It was better than any music ever downloaded onto my iPod. In fact, when Finger's bike ploughed into the water, the people in the main streets of Gawler could have heard him cursing.

"Yesss!" cheered Jack, punching the air.

We reined in the horses, turned and gazed back at the dam. The bikes had disappeared under the water and four wet mud-splattered figures were dragging themselves onto the bank.

"You'll pay for this!" shrilled Meathead in his squeaky little girl voice. "You'll pay big time!"

Not wanting to hear how he intended to make us pay, we trotted the horses away from the dam.

"Guess that'll hold them for a while," said Sarah, her grin as wide as a paddock fence. "They shouldn't get too far before the police arrive."

"Hey, look!" I pointed ahead. Down the path, heading toward us, rattling and rumbling in protest, came the professor's trusty old ute. Such a friendly sight. I felt like hugging the driver.

And there was Arty. Hair matted with blood, a jagged

cut on his forehead and one eye almost closed. He hung out the passenger side window and waved to us. "Everyone okay?"

"We are now," I said grinning at him.

"I think you'll find who you're looking for in the dam," said Noah with a laugh. "They went for an unplanned swim on their bikes."

"You mean…" A satisfied smile spread slowly across Arty's battered face.

"He means Meathead, Fingers, and their biker friends won't be going anywhere in a hurry."

"Oh yes they will." The professor smirked. "They will be going to jail. About five minutes after you children took off, the police arrived. They rescued Arty and took Simpson off to headquarters for questioning. And there are two patrol cars directly behind us."

As if on cue, police sirens could be heard approaching. Fast. Red and blue lights jittered and flashed as they drew nearer. I looked across at the dam and grinned. Four muddy figures were trying to bolt in four different directions.

"Gotta go," shouted Arty, dangling a pair of handcuffs out the window. "Got a score to settle. Come on, Gramps. Rounding this lot up should be more fun than a ride on the roller-coaster at Dreamworld."

"Need any help?" asked Noah, his eyes even shinier than Jack's.

Was this the same boy who'd hidden in the tree and let

me take the rap for trespassing?

"Can we? Can we?" gabbled Jack, leaning forward on his horse's neck. "Please…"

"You've done your share," replied Arty. Then seeing the despondent look on the boys' faces, he added, "You've got the important job of telling the police what happened and directing them to the dam. I wouldn't want any of those scumbags to get away."

With that, the professor's ute backfired, did a couple of bunny-hops, then shot after one of the fleeing criminals.

We sat on our horses and watched. By the time the police cars pulled up beside us, Arty and the professor had already collected two of the runners, handcuffed them to a bar in the tray of the ute and were zeroing in on a third.

"Any left to catch?" asked a young constable leaning from the police car window.

Sarah pointed toward the dam. "One guy circled back and I think he's hiding up that tree."

I slipped off Noah's horse and grinned at Sarah. "Shall we?" Without a word she leant down and pulled me up behind her. With me bumping on her horse's rump we trotted over to the tree in question and stopped underneath.

"Can you smell something stinky?" I asked Sarah, screwing up my nose and pulling a face. "You know—like sweaty armpits?"

"Smells more like dog's poop to me."

I took another sniff. "You know, I reckon it smells like

rotten maggoty meat that's been left hanging in a tree too long."

At the same time as Meathead let out a string of four-letter words that would curdle cream, the police car screamed up beside us.

"Okay, girls. We'll take over now."

The last we heard from Meathead was when the sergeant led him handcuffed to the police car. His squeaky oaths could still be heard as the police car took off, sirens wailing, heading for the police station.

19

TREEHAVEN CROSS-COUNTRY
—2012—
SUPERHEROES.

I paused in the act of polishing the trophy on top of our television and grinned. It was a large silver trophy with a statue of a horse and rider leaping over water.

On Cross-Country day, our team—*The Super-heroes*—had been totally awesome. Jack and Sarah flew around the course like champs and even Tayla and I managed to jump everything without falling off once. Of course, after being chased by Meathead's bikers, Kate's Cross-Country course seemed like a baby event.

Six weeks had passed since wrapping up (that's P.I. talk) the Big Egg mystery. Simpson and his buddies were in jail. Arty received a pat on the back and a promotion from his boss. And I'd finished writing my latest true-crime story, *'Rebecca Turnbull P.I.: The Mystery of the Stolen Dinosaur Egg.'* It was published in *Kidlit* magazine on the internet.

Rebecca Turnbull, my fictional P.I. character was one cool babe. Instead of hiding in a cupboard like me, she'd kicked butt throughout the mystery. With the help of her lethal Doberman, Fang, she'd overpowered Fingers and Meathead in the time it would take me to brush my teeth. However, Rebecca had one huge advantage over me. She had no mother in her story. No mother to ground her. No mother to wildly chop potatoes under her nose. No mother to send her off to ride wild mustangs instead of solving a mystery.

"Will you take a look at these?" It was Mum, frowning into the oval mirror on our lounge room wall. "Six more grey hairs." She turned to me. "And who do I have to thank for them?"

Ha. There was no way I was going to answer *that* question. Instead I went back to polishing the trophy.

"I guess it's Chiana's fault." Sarah's sugary sweet voice didn't match the cat's bum face she pulled at me.

Then, after putting her face back in order, she carefully adjusted her boob tube and arranged herself on the edge of the lounge chair. No lolling back and stretching her legs for Sarah—she might disturb the lines of her new leather skirt.

Mum's frown deepened. She whipped around and glared at my step-sibling. "And what about you, Madam? Half of these grey hairs are due to *you* turning into one of Cha's gung-ho side-kicks."

Under cover of itching my nose, I poked my tongue out

at Sarah and crossed my eyes until everything went blurry and out of shape.

So there!

Still smiling, I bent down and tickled Leroy's tummy. His lips dribbled into an ecstatic loose grin. Actually, everything about poor Leroy was loose after two weeks of his draconian diet. Maybe I should buy him a packet of black jellybeans next time I went to the shop. Just for special occasions.

"Let's go." Ken, dressed in his best navy suit and sky blue shirt, bustled into the room, picked up the car keys from the coffee-table and swung them around on one finger.

"Come on, Marg. Stop worrying about your hair. It's perfect," he said. "Professor Goodenough is officially returning the stolen dinosaur egg to the museum at two o'clock. We don't want to be late."

An hour later, standing in front of the *Addyman Plesiosaur,* I watched the professor shuffle up to the microphone. His beard and hair had been detangled, shampooed and trimmed and although he wore a coat that swirled around his ankles, on the scale of scruffy it only hit a five. While the professor adjusted the height of the microphone, I caught a glimpse of a little black nose and two bright button eyes as Pedro peeped out from one of the coat's many pockets.

"Today, I am returning my father's fossilized *Therizinosaur* to the museum," the professor began, pushing Pedro's head down out of sight. "But first, I would like to thank my grandson, P.C. Arthur Goodenough, for his courage, and Chiana Ryan and her friends for saving my egg. And now, Chiana, would you like to come up and give a little speech then perform the official duty of placing the *Therizinosaur* back in its rightful place?"

Me? Geez. I'd rather face Barnaby without a carrot than go up to the microphone and speak. If only the one hundred and twenty million year old dinosaur standing behind me wasn't so bony, I'd sneak in behind him and hide.

Sarah dug me in the ribs and whispered. "I told you to wear your purple top and lime-green nail polish. But no—you never listen to me."

I ignored Sarah. After all, I was wearing my new jeans. The jeans Mum insisted I wear—even though they made me feel like I had two planks of wood strapped to my legs. You know, the sort of jeans that needed a week or two buried in a muddy puddle of water to make them wearable.

I could see Jack, Noah and Tayla grinning wildly as they clapped and whistled, urging me on. Suddenly a lump jammed my throat and I had to swallow hard to work it free. I was so totally proud of my assistants. Even sucky Sarah. Without them, the dinosaur egg wouldn't be with the professor today.

Jack and Noah gave me the thumbs-up sign as I walked up to the microphone, while Arty, dressed in his police uniform, winked at me. The cuts and bruises on his face had healed. His hair, now clean, shiny and thick made him look like a movie star.

I took the box containing the *Therizinosaur* from the professor's hands and stood on tiptoe to speak.

"This little guy says thanks to Arty for rescuing him," I said, holding up the box. "And the credit for keeping him safe from the bad guys goes to my best friends Jack and Tayla, my new friend, Noah, and my sister Sarah. Thank you."

With that, I clumped toward the empty stand with *'Fossilized Dinosaur Egg discovered by Professor Cyril Goodenough on 8th September 1934'*, engraved on the bottom. I carefully opened the box and then gaped in confusion. There was no fossilized egg inside. Instead there were egg shells and what looked like a newly hatched baby echidna. Had the professor become so absent-minded he didn't know the difference between a real egg and a fossilized one?

I glanced up, my mind whirling. A smile lit the professor's face as he caught my eye.

"She's called Chiana—and she's yours. It's my way of saying thank you."

"Mine?"

I looked across at Mum, my heart in my eyes. Mum's face had that shocked bloodless look. You know, the sort of look traumatized cyclone victims have when their house blows away. I got the feeling Mum didn't think a pet echidna was a good idea.

"Of course echidnas are a protected species," went on the professor. "Which means little Chiana will have to stay at the sanctuary with me. But you're welcome to visit your namesake in the Chiana Ryan Enclosure whenever you feel like it."

"Wow! The Chiana Ryan Enclosure!"

Arty gave his grandfather a nudge.

"The echidna-enclosure also has newly hatched babies called Jack, Noah, Sarah and Tayla," added the professor.

"What about Leroy?" I asked.

"Leroy?"

"My other assistant."

The professor's expression remained puzzled.

"Her dog," supplied Mum, rolling her eyes heavenwards.

"Whatever." The professor, smirking at his weird teenage-talk, dug a hand into one of his many pockets and pulled out the real grey fossilized egg. "Now, would you like to continue with the ceremony?"

Taking a step forward, I gently settled the mega-million-year-old dinosaur egg on top of the empty stand.

And then I let out a deep contented sigh.

The museum smelled of dust. Of old dead things. Of dry stuffed animals with blank staring eyes.

And the little *Therizinosaur* had returned home.

About the Author

A former school teacher and greyhound trainer, June has always dreamed of being an author. She wrote her first full-length story (with chapters) when she was nine-years-old—'Donald McDonald in Texas'—a story involving a rather extraordinary boy who rode buck-jumpers in a rodeo. And when she penned her first murder mystery, 'Murder Behind Bars', it resulted in her fifth-grade teacher questioning her home life. ☺

Even now, in retirement, June's favorite place to be is sitting in front of her computer, making up stories.